The Witch of the Highlands

Azusa

Battle with me, Lady Azusa!

Don't come crying to me if you get hurt.

©Beni

I've Been Killing SLIMES for 300 Years and Maxed Out My Level 4

Kisetsu Morita

Illustration by **Benio**

YEN ON

NEW YORK

I've Been Killing SLIMES for 300 Years and Maxed Out My Level 4

KISETSU MORITA

Translation by Jasmine Bernhardt
Cover art by Benio

This book is a work of fiction. Names, characters, places, and incidents are
the product of the author's imagination or are used fictitiously. Any resemblance
to actual events, locales, or persons, living or dead, is coincidental.

SLIME TAOSHITE SANBYAKUNEN, SHIRANAIUCHINI
LEVEL MAX NI NATTEMASHITA vol. 4
Copyright © 2017 Kisetsu Morita
Illustrations copyright © 2017 Benio
All rights reserved.
Original Japanese edition published in 2017 by SB Creative Corp.

This English edition is published by arrangement with SB Creative Corp., Tokyo
in care of Tuttle-Mori Agency, Inc., Tokyo.

English translation © 2019 by Yen Press, LLC

Yen On
1290 Avenue of the Americas
New York, NY 10104

Visit us at yenpress.com
facebook.com/yenpress
twitter.com/yenpress
yenpress.tumblr.com
instagram.com/yenpress

First Yen On Edition: April 2019

Yen On is an imprint of Yen Press, LLC.
The Yen On name and logo are trademarks of Yen Press, LLC.

The publisher is not responsible for websites (or their content) that are not
owned by the publisher.

Library of Congress Cataloging-in-Publication Data
Names: Morita, Kisetsu, author. | Benio, illustrator. | Engel, Taylor, translator. | Bernhardt, Jasmine, translator
Title: I've been killing slimes for 300 years and maxed out my level / Kisetsu Morita ; illustration by Benio.
Other titles: Slime taoshite sanbyakunen, shiranaiuchini level max ni nattemashita. English |
I have been killing slimes for 300 years
Description: First Yen On edition. | New York : Yen On, 2018– |
v. 1–2: translation by Taylor Engel. | v. 3–4: translation by Jasmine Bernhardt
Identifiers: LCCN 2017059843 | ISBN 9780316448277 (v. 1 : pbk.) | ISBN 9780316448291 (v. 2 : pbk.) |
ISBN 9781975329310 (v. 3 : pbk.) | ISBN 9781975382636 (v. 4 : pbk.)
Subjects: CYAC: Reincarnation—Fiction. | Witches—Fiction.
Classification: LCC PZ7.1.M6725 Iv 2018 | DDC [Fic]—dc23
LC record available at https://lccn.loc.gov/2017059843

ISBNs: 978-1-9753-8263-6 (paperback)
978-1-9753-8264-3 (ebook)

1 3 5 7 9 10 8 6 4 2

LSC-C

Printed in the United States of America

Contents

Story by Kisetsu Morita Illustration by Benio

She slaughtered slimes for 300 years...

I ATE A **MUSHROOM** AND TURNED INTO A **KID**

It was a beautiful day.

"Wow, the sky is so clear!"

The light pouring in through the window was lovely, and I felt like going out for a picnic. We lived in the highlands, so we were kind of already in a good picnicking spot.

"Madam Teacher, the weather really is gorgeous today! It's days like these we should cook outside!" Halkara the elf was also relatively excited. She was off from work at the factory that day, so she'd slept in longer than normal.

"Cooking outside can only mean one thing! Meat!"

"Meat! Meat! Meat!"

With their gleaming eyes, our dragon duo of Laika and Flatorte seemed more like a zombie duo.

It hadn't been all that long since we had our last barbecue, but they didn't seem tired of it yet.

"No, we're not grilling meat. This will be a mushroom cookout."

Halkara spoke with the utmost seriousness. Well, mushrooms were on the list of things to grill during cookouts, but it was a little weird to have *only* mushrooms. It was like eating ramen without the noodles.

"Where I'm from, everyone would gather various types of mushrooms and just cook all of them. We called it a mushroom cookout, or a mushout for short. The ladies enjoy it because it's so healthy."

It was hard to tell where the jokes stopped and the facts began. But it probably wouldn't hurt to give it a shot just this once. "Do you even have mushrooms?"

"Indeed, I do. I have the ones I've been raising, and I'll gather the rest from the forest. I will be back in about an hour and a half with a basket full of them."

Halkara was weirdly knowledgeable about mushrooms, so I didn't have any reason not to believe her.

"Then you'll be on time for lunch, no problem. All right, we'll have a mushout, then."

"Yay! This is gonna be fun!"

"I read the hermits of old would go into the mountains and keep themselves alive on just a few grasses. They wouldn't even ingest wheat. This will be an ascetic meal."

My daughters were getting excited, too.

And, Shalsha, this isn't going to feel like a religious meal.

The two dragons didn't seem all that into it, but what could I do about that? In a way, a mushroom barbecue was a rarer opportunity than a meat barbecue, so they'd just have to deal.

"Oh well. I guess I could make a hamburger full of mushrooms!" Flatorte mentioned a way to cheat without breaking the mushroom restriction. Mushroom dishes were fine, then? I mean, they were free to eat meat, sure... But then the mushrooms wouldn't be the centerpiece.

"Well then, I am off to gather mushrooms!" Halkara shot her right hand up into the air, still just as excited as before.

"Okay. Oh... And just one thing I want you to be mindful of: Please don't bring back any poisonous mushrooms..." I was confident in Halkara's knowledge, but her execution could be a little sloppy. Sorting out poisonous mushrooms from the rest sometimes got complicated. Well, more than sometimes. Pretty often, actually.

"I'll be careful. I have completely memorized all the edible and inedible mushrooms of the nearby woods! It won't be a problem at all!"

"Yeah, but now I'm even more concerned, so be sure to double-check before you put them on the grill..."

I knew if we checked before frying them, we wouldn't end up cooking a poisonous one by mistake.

An hour and a half later...

Halkara returned with a basket full of mushrooms.

"All right! I've chosen edible mushrooms and *only* edible mushrooms! We will all be just fine!"

"Okay. I'll trust you if you say so. I'll give them a taste before my daughters eat."

"You don't trust me at all!"

I mean, I couldn't help it. Nothing was ever truly certain, and people who spoke in absolutes always ended up in doubt.

"We'll do a thorough check. Just a check. Companies that take care to check things avoid the biggest incidents. Messy employee management makes for a bad company."

"It sounds like you've seen it all before, Madam Teacher..."

In my past life, I witnessed lots of news stories about company higher-ups who apologized for mistakes and accidents due to the employees' carelessness. There's a lot of administrative responsibility that comes along with that.

"Then I'll go to my room next and pick some of the mushrooms I'm cultivating!"

Halkara collected a wide variety of mushrooms and cultivated them in her room since she used them for herbal medicines. That made her room look a little suspect, but it wasn't much different from my drying plants for poultices as a witch.

"Sure, sure. Do what you like. I'll leave you in charge today, Halkara."

"He-he-he, I'll show you what high-quality mushrooms can do!"

Halkara announced like a character from a cooking manga before heading to her room.

◇

And then, lunchtime.

We placed a table and chairs outside and started cooking.

"Ta-daaa! I've collected quite a variety of mushrooms!"

Sure enough, there were white ones, black ones, and red ones. Some looked like eggs, some like umbrellas, and some just like sticks.

"None of them is poisonous, so we'll be all right. We'll fry them in butter on a griddle then drizzle some elvin on top, and that's it! It's sooo good!"

Elvin was kind of like soy sauce.

Butter–soy sauce mushrooms, huh? That actually sounded delicious. It would probably go really well with some beer, so I got a bit of that ready, too.

"Mistress, you're drinking during the day?" Flatorte queried. It was a little embarrassing being asked outright like that.

"Why not? Halkara's off today, so I should be safe if I finish after lunch."

And so our mushout began.

"First, we'll start with a gnome's hideout, as is tradition."

"Wait, that's a name I've never heard before." *Gnome* was the name of a tiny race.

"It's not native to this area, so I'm growing some in my room. It's called that because it's just big enough for little gnomes to hide in. It has the quintessential mushroom flavor."

I gave it a taste, and she was right. It tasted like a stronger shiitake. And the butter–soy sauce went so well with it! And wow, the beer went even better with it!!

"Phew! I could go for another glass! This is delicious!"

Man, day drinking is the best! Mushrooms are the best!

The other mushrooms were, of course, delicious. The butter-and-soy-sauce combination was so good. It made everything better.

"This is a black dwarf. It tastes the best right before it gets too big. I picked out these mushrooms very carefully."

"Mm. Delicious." Even Shalsha, who wasn't the biggest fan of vegetables, seemed satisfied as she ate.

Even Laika the carnivore said, "This isn't too bad," as she stabbed her fork into the mushrooms.

Everyone's so into it. I'm glad we had this mushout.

"I never knew there were so many kinds of mushrooms! The forest is full of mysteries! This is so cool!" Falfa gave her compliments to the forest itself.

She was right; it was a fascinating part of the woods that we never usually paid attention to.

"How is everything, Madam Teacher? See? Nothing I've collected is poisonous."

"You're right. I'm sorry for doubting you."

It was nice to know that she actually wouldn't end up putting poisonous ones in the mix if I cautioned her enough.

"What about this red one?" I asked as I popped the new species into my mouth.

"Oh, that's also a gnome's hideout... Wait, no, actually, that's a gnomesform."

"Huh, that's another funny name."

"Yes, it's a poisonous one that's said to shrink whoever eats it."

"Wow, so it's a poisonous— Wait, hold on."

Expressionless, I clapped my hands onto Halkara's shoulders.

"Did you say poisonous just now? You said it was poisonous, didn't you?"

"Erm, Madam Teacher, your eyes are scaring me…"

"And I told you *so* many times to be careful what mushrooms you pick from the woods…"

"Oh no! I picked what I got from the forest very carefully! But I guess I ended up picking some inedible ones from the batches I'm growing in my room!"

"So?! You think I'm fine with that just because you didn't get them from the forest?!"

I'd let my guard down. I'd underestimated how much of a ditz Halkara was…

"Are you all right, Mom? I'll take you to bed if you feel sick." Shalsha came up beside me with an uneasy expression. My daughter's care and attention warmed my heart.

"More importantly, you and Falfa didn't have any of this, did you?"

Shalsha shook her head. Falfa, in the background, did the same.

The two of them appeared as young girls, so we took great care around them.

And Laika and Flatorte were dragons, so frankly, they weren't weak enough to succumb to a single poisonous mushroom.

Halkara knew how to handle these things, so she would be fine. Rosalie couldn't die, being a ghost and all, and she didn't eat to begin with. No problems there.

Stats-wise, a poisonous mushroom wasn't enough to kill me, so I guess I could say that I'd avoided the worst.

At the moment, I didn't have any obvious symptoms.

"So? What's the gnomesform's poison like?"

"Er, well… It's a very odd sort of mushroom. I've heard it makes you like a gnome…"

"So it shrinks you? No way eating a mushroom could do something like that to—"

Something strange was clearly happening in my body.

I felt like I was floating.

It was like I'd gotten a sudden fever...

Then, for about ten seconds, I lost consciousness—

I opened my eyes.

The first thing I felt was how baggy my clothes were. My hat sat over my whole face. When I moved it out of the way, Halkara seemed enormous. *Wait. Something's weird with my perception, and everything looks just a bit too far away.*

Both Laika and Rosalie also seemed huge. Everyone looked like my older sisters. Even Shalsha seemed big. When did she get so mature? Did she have a growth spurt?

Shalsha blinked at me. That was a level of surprise I'd never seen on her face before.

Then, suddenly, someone squeezed me from behind.

"Eee! You're so cute! You're so cute, Mommy!"

Oh, that voice was Falfa's. But I could feel myself being lifted into the air. *When did she get this strong?* Was this also a skill from a growth spurt?

"You're a hundred and fifty times cuter than I am, Falfa. But hearing you call me cute makes me happy."

"Yeah, you got even cuter, Mommy!"

That's strange. Did I put that much effort into my makeup today?

By the way, since I'd been keeping my seventeen-year-old figure for three hundred years, my skin was still supple. When it came to makeup, I didn't have to apply much to achieve a natural look; all I had to do was slap a little on and that was that. But that's a different story.

Laika then rushed over. She really did seem much bigger now.

"Laika, my sense of perspective is way off."

"Lady Azusa... Have you not realized it yet?"

I'd long been aware of how cute my daughters were, but that probably wasn't what she was talking about.

"Lady Azusa, you've gotten smaller... You're perhaps the size of a five- or six-year-old child..."

"……"

Once again, I looked at my baggy clothes.

"…Gaaaaahhh! What the heck?! I'm the same size as that detective kid now!"

"Lady Azusa, you are not a detective or anything of the sort! Unless… Have you also gone mad?!"

Oh, I'm totally mentally sound, actually.

◇

I rushed back to my house in the highlands, and the first thing I did was find a mirror.

Staring back at me was a little kid.

"I'm a child…"

"Yes. Looking the way you do, you might even be a toddler."

I was thankful that Laika could remain calm at times like these.

If you were wondering, Halkara had bowed in apology to me several times then shut herself in her room to research a way to bring me back to normal.

We tried casting a Cure Poison spell, but the effect that shrank me had already been activated and run its course, so it was ineffective. It wasn't like my strength was being chipped away from me in the present tense…

The mushroom was called "gnomesform," and eating it made me look like this. I guess it was true to its name.

As long as there wasn't any more poison in it, I should be fine for now.

"I hope I can get back to normal soon. I don't really have clothes for this body in the long term, so that's a problem."

"Erm, Lady Azusa…?" Laika was pressing her hand gently to her mouth.

Was she sympathizing with my misery?

"Ah… This might come across as rude, but please allow me to say this to you. You— You're cute… You're absolutely adorable."

Should I be happy about this…?

Then a very cheery Flatorte arrived.

I had a bad feeling about it, but I moved too slowly to escape.

"Hawww, you're so cute! You're so cute, Mistress! Aaand up we go! Aaaaand up!"

"Don't lift me like that! And I'm not *actually* a kid! I'm really not into this! The way you're just throwing me around is seriously freaking me out!"

In the end, I became a rag doll for my family to play with…

Afterward, Laika went to Flatta and purchased some children's clothes, which I was wearing now. She even found a miniature version of my hat for me to wear. With the new clothes, I ended up looking like my usual self, just bite-size.

"Okay, Mommy. Say ahhh!"

As I sat on the floor, Falfa brought over a cookie.

"Don't treat me like a child—wait, I guess I am…" I opened my mouth, and she shoved it in.

Mm, good stuff. I did have some conflicting feelings about the experience, though.

Then Shalsha came over, hefting a very thick book. "Today I will be doing a reading designed for children."

"Yep, that's me. I sure am a children."

"I'll be reading you the first volume of the Records of Meditation, *Fundamental Discrepancies Between Knowledge and Experience.* This is an in-depth discussion of intuitive cognition—a true masterpiece."

"Haven't you set the bar a little too high…?"

"You'll get sleepy as I read to you. It's perfect for a young child's nap time."

I feel like her reasoning is a little off, but I can play along, I suppose…

After that, Shalsha started telling me about how "Intuitive cognition is not caused by an accumulation of knowledge," among other things, but that went over my head.

I got sleepier and sleepier. Could my response be more childlike than normal? Or was it really because the book was super boring?

I started nodding off as I sat leaning against the wall.

Then Falfa snuggled up beside me. "You're so cute, Mommy. I'll nap with you."

"Okay... I'm just... so sleepy... So, so sleepy..."

I almost wanted to fall asleep right on the spot, but Shalsha suddenly stood up—

"Yah! You must awaken to spirituality!"

—and gave me a little chop!

"Hey, come on. Don't wake me up..."

"This is the very definition of intuitive cognition. This is something that can only be awakened by experience."

Was she mad because I'd gotten sleepy while she was reading?

"But...sleeping is an experience as well... I, Shalsha, shall allow it."

So she was letting us sleep anyway.

"After all, I'm sleepy, too..."

She snuggled up to me on my other side, and for a short while, the three of us dozed.

Times like these weren't so bad.

Then something a bit unusual happened during dinnertime.

There was a strange flag planted at the peak of my omelet.

"...This is what you do for a kid's lunch!"

"What do you think? I decided to make your meal a little fancier to suit your looks, Lady Azusa!" Laika's expression told me she was proud of her creation.

"You guys are having way too much fun with me..."

Hopefully I wouldn't have to weather the kiddie jokes for much longer.

I anticipated the punch being something about how tight my clothes would be in the morning.

"…Laika, don't you have a lot more food than normal?"

"No, I almost have less than normal. I see your appetite has gotten smaller."

That made sense. In a way, my metabolism was better in this body.

Above me, Rosalie said, "Ah, so the weight of the soul stays the same even if the body gets smaller!" Not sure how she measured that.

"Halkara isn't here, though."

"Miss Halkara said she would be doing some research and has locked herself in her room all day."

I had a bad feeling about that. *No, don't tell me, don't tell me…*

"Erm, Lady Azusa, I have one request to make." Laika seemed to be somewhat impatient, like she couldn't hold back her joy.

"Yes, what is it?"

"I know these might be bad manners during a meal, but…might I be allowed to pat your head?"

With hollow eyes, I sighed. "…Fine, just dote on me all you want! I'm ready for it!"

Soon after, Laika started patting my head. But I got the general impression that she was hesitant. I guess this was new for her. When I did the same to my daughters, I ruffled their hair relentlessly.

"And? You satisfied now?"

I was sullenly eating my dinner. Laika sat beside me.

"I feel like I now understand a little of how you feel about your daughters… Oh, you're much too adorable… And that sulk on your face is much too cute…"

Right, little girls were cute, no matter the expression they wore. Even if they suddenly started talking about politics, the abrupt disparity between their face and the topic would be endearing in its own way.

Then Flatorte also stopped eating and came to pat me with a "You can't hog her, Laika!" It didn't matter who pet me anymore.

"I know for certain that I, Flatorte, am patting you more gently. Isn't this much softer than what Laika was doing?"

You're getting competitive over this, too?

"Mommy, Falfa wants a little brother or sister. Oh, Shalsha's my twin, so she doesn't count."

"And for Shalsha's own growth, I would like more opportunities to interact with younger children."

Waitwaitwaitwait, are they telling me to have kids...? I'm not even married!

Rosalie then floated down to admonish them. "That's not possible, you two."

Exactly! You tell them!

"First, she has to search for a suitable partner to court."

This isn't a question of procedure!

"Let's see—of the people I know, there's Krewed the ghost. Oh, and Balter the vengeful spirit is very handsome, too."

"Why are you naming dead people?!"

Well, it would be lovely to have more adorable children like Falfa and Shalsha around, but I certainly didn't have any plans for that. Could there be another child in this world as cute as they were? Probably not.

I started eating the side salad as I thought about all that. Compared to its usual flavor, it was incredibly bitter. Hmm, maybe kids never finished their vegetables because they were more sensitive to bitter tastes than adults.

Then Halkara appeared.

"I'm sorry I'm late!" Her expression was lucid, like she'd been freed from an evil spirit possessing her.

"Oh, did you figure out a way to return me to normal?!"

Halkara then fell to her knees before me and bowed her head.

"I have no idea how to return you to normal; please forgive me!"

"Then why did you look so pleased with yourself?!"

"Once I made up my mind to confess everything and apologize, I felt much better! I don't have a single hint or the slightest clue of how to fix this! I'm just sorry! So very sorry!"

Apologizing to me isn't going to solve anything!

"Well, there's no problem at all, Mistress!" Flatorte crossed her arms, determined. "We can raise you for the next twelve years or so, and then you'll be back to your original form."

That's way too long to solve this problem!

I didn't have much other choice at this point. We were almost out of options.

"We'll ask the demons. We helped them search for the undead last time, so they'll probably lend us a hand. Actually, we'll force them to."

I *was* going to try the spell for summoning Beelzebub, but if my pronunciation was off, I ran the risk of landing her in the bathtub, so after I warmed the bathwater, I went outside and drew a magic circle.

"Lady Azusa, it's much too dangerous to go out alone this late."

"I guarantee there won't be any perverts out here in the highlands."

It was a huge pain drawing a magic circle. Having a child's body made drawing certain spots needlessly complicated.

"Vosanosanonnjishidow veiani enlira!"

As I intoned the spell, a black mist appeared around me, but Beelzebub didn't appear.

Believing all was well, I went back inside. I glanced around, but no Beelzebub.

Was my small frame not enough for the magic…?

Thirty minutes later, Beelzebub, looking warm and refreshed, strolled into the dining room.

"What a lovely bath! ♪"

"At least tell me you appeared in the bath!"

Us summoning you means it's an emergency, you know. But I did go out of my way to prepare the bath, so that doesn't sound very convincing.

"Hmm…? Who are you? You look quite similar to Azusa, though…

Don't tell me you're her biological daughter...? Oh no, I don't think I should ask that..."

I could tell she was getting all the wrong ideas again, but considering my form, I couldn't do much about that...

"No, it's me. It's me, Azusa!"

I pointed to my face and claimed my person.

"Oh-ho, I see you have a tradition in your land of naming children after their parents."

"Noooo, nonono, I'm not Azusa the Second; I'm Azusa the First! Azusa, Witch of the Highlands! I'm all small because of a poisonous mushroom!"

There was an uncomfortable silence.

Beelzebub then suddenly hoisted me into the air.

"What a cuuutie! How adorable you are! This is a dangerous sort of cute!"

"Hey, put me down! Put me down! I hate being treated like a kid, so stop it!"

"And insisting you hate being treated like a kid only makes you a manipulative sort of cute!"

No! I really am still an adult on the inside! "And since we don't know how to turn me back to normal, I want to borrow the demons' knowledge and network."

"I see. So that's why you summoned me."

Still aloft, I nodded.

It didn't seem like my stats had gone down with my size (if they did, then I wouldn't have succeeded in summoning Beelzebub), so I could probably get out of her grip if I resisted, but I couldn't help looking helpless. Might as well play the part.

"There is a possibility we may find some information if we searched around Vanzeld Castle."

"Right! So do something. I can't stay like this forever!"

"...Would you?"

What's that supposed to mean?

"It wouldn't be so terrible to lead a life as the strongest child, would it? I never believed I would ever see this side of you."

Oh no! She's trying to keep things as they are!

"You may also become my adopted daughter in lieu of Falfa or Shalsha. You will receive a proper education for gifted children."

I'm not asking for any of that! "Okay, then I'll spread the word that the great demon Beelzebub lost to a little girl once."

"What?! That's not fair! It's dirty, I tell you!"

"I'll play dirty if I have to in order to get back to normal!"

Beelzebub's face was scrunched up in frustration, but she finally seemed to give in. "Very well. However, I won't make much progress without you, so I am taking you along with me to Vanzeld Castle."

"Fine by me. You might have to examine me anyway."

"And we will bring Shalsha and Falfa along as well."

"Sure, that's fine… But why?"

Dead serious, Beelzebub replied:

"Because it makes me happy."

Afterward, we called on Fatla the leviathan, and in her huge carrier form, she transported my two daughters, Beelzebub, and me to the demon lands.

And while we were on the move, Beelzebub was spoiling me rotten. She gave me all the different kinds of candy and sweets that existed in this world, even a cookie house.

Which, by the way, Beelzebub had forced our skilled chef, Vania, into making. When she brought it over, I could see the exhaustion on her face. "Boss, I'm telling you: The schedule this time is too unreasonable… Aren't you skipping an important meeting right now…?"

"And thus, I've reported that I have an urgent matter I cannot ignore. I've done all the paperwork, so there's no problem."

"I guess that's fine… Please enjoy the sweets. I'm especially proud of the pudding I made today."

It was a firm, springy pudding. I took a spoonful and put it in my mouth. "Mm, it's so good! I guess my taste buds are more childlike, because it tastes even yummier than usual!"

My daughters seemed to be greatly pleased by it, as well.

"It's good; it's soooooo good!"

"Delicious. It's like I'm dreaming."

As she watched us, Beelzebub said, "What a lovely sight. The loveliest sight in the world, if I may say so." Hearing those words in reference to me was pretty unnerving, honestly.

We even took a bath together and all slept side by side in the same bed. There were four of us, so it wasn't a comfortable fit, though.

I slept with both Falfa and Beelzebub clinging to me, and Shalsha was snuggled right up to Beelzebub, like she was hugging a big tree.

"Ahhh, I'm in heaven! I'm in heaven! It's like an adorable explosion!"

A demon shouldn't be yelling about heaven…

In the end, Beelzebub spent our entire time on board (well, on Fatla, not on a battleship or something) fawning over me, and we finally came to the landing spot near Vanzeld Castle.

Just before we landed, Beelzebub was squeezing me tightly as she sat.

"Uh, I'm not a stuffed animal, you know…"

"Landing can be quite rough. I cannot have you swaying about and falling over."

"It's not *that* dangerous. I think you're already well aware of how strong I am…"

"That's that. This is different! When we get to the castle, I have a national conference I need to attend, so we'll be very far apart, but I want you to be a good girl, okay?"

Is this demon seriously going to prioritize me over a national conference?

It would be weird for me to complain since I asked for her help, but wasn't that just a bad idea?

"Shalsha, Falfa, I trust you two to look after Azusa."

"Okay! We'll look after Mommy!"

"We will make sure that she doesn't eat too much candy."

The two were answering in earnest. *Wait, come on! I might be small, but I'm still your mom!*

"Mommy, do you need to go potty?"

"Tell me if you get thirsty. Toddlers are small, so it's very easy for them to get dehydrated. And slime bodies are made up of ninety-nine percent water."

I was a total child to them.

And I didn't know slimes were like jellyfish… They were almost entirely water.

It seemed like when someone became small, they were treated like a kid as a matter of course.

I wasn't angry or resentful, but there were some things I just didn't get. Still, if I complained in the body I had now, I could predict that they'd respond to me like I was a whiny child. I was cornered.

"All right! Let's find a way to turn me back into an adult!"

"You're so adorable when you act like a grown-up, Azusa!"

"She's at the age when she wants to deny that she is a child—the first rebellious stage."

Shalsha, my own child, was even giving a weird analysis of me.

Hey! I'm actually *an adult, you know! What's weird here is your reaction!*

But the majority favored their logic, so what could I do?

Falfa and Shalsha took my hands, and we alighted from Fatla.

Beelzebub literally flew off to her conference (like she was putting me first as long as she possibly could), and Fatla and Vania showed us into the castle.

Here we were again at Vanzeld Castle. I was starting to get a feel for where everything was inside.

"First, please head to the castle's guest room. We've already picked up several specialists, so I will introduce you to them."

"Thanks. I appreciate it."

Even though I was small, Fatla was still treating me as professionally as she always did. Her personality was more obvious at times like these. "Also, please refrain from walking about outside too much."

"What? Nobody around here is going to eat human children, are they?"

"That is not the case, but…if the demon king finds you, I cannot say that there won't be unnecessary commotion as a result…" Fatla chose her words carefully until she finally got across what she was trying to say.

"Oh… If Pecora finds me, we'll definitely have complications…"

I still didn't know how to handle her very well.

In a word, she was selfish. And she loved practical jokes.

Maybe it was a given for the demon king, but she toyed with everyone around her like it was no big deal. I didn't want her pushing me around. She was the type to always put her own interests ahead of anyone else's.

"Vania, just in case, check to see that Her Majesty isn't in the hallway ahead of us."

"Yes, understood!"

Vania clomped off in an incredibly awkward fashion. I wasn't confident that she'd ever get ahead in life. And even if she did succeed, she'd probably cause a scandal and end up demoted…

"I wonder if she'll ever get rid of those, you know…featherbrained tendencies of hers." Without her little sister around, the elder sister vented her honest opinion. "I believed for at least a hundred years that she could do anything she put her mind to, but maybe she can't do anything at all…"

Ohhh. I was an only child, but I understand Fatla's pain!

After a moment, Vania came back. "It's all right! I see neither hide nor hair of Her Majesty!"

"Vania, keep your voice down! Someone will hear you!"

After a typical Vania screwup, we walked along briskly. The three strange kids must have stood out, but acting extra suspicious would've drawn more attention. We proceeded with no apparent concern.

Then we finally came to the room we were supposed to hide in.

"Phew, guess we made it this far."

"You don't stand out at all, Mommy, since you're so small."

"They say there used to be scouts who took advantage of their small stature. This is another application of that principle."

My two daughters seemed awfully crafty.

All right then, time to open the door!

"...Wait, you're kidding me. I can't reach..."

The doorknob was much higher than I thought, and I couldn't turn it!

I jumped, but I still couldn't get a grip!

"Aha-ha-ha-ha!"

"Vania, it's rude to laugh. She's our guest—even if you find it funny, keep it to yourself... *Pfffft...*"

The leviathans are laughing at me!

Geez, how insulting! But it was true that I was acting funny, so it'd be weird of me to hate them. If I was going to hold a grudge against anyone, it would be the one who created this whole mess—right, Halkara. *Dammit, Halkara!*

"Okay, Falfa will open it, then!"

Falfa stood on her toes and managed to open the door.

This building doesn't score well for accessibility. Keep your doors low enough for kids to open.

I proceeded through the door that Falfa opened.

"*Sigh*, we finally made it!"

"You seem well, Elder Sister. ♪"

It was the last voice I wanted to hear.

Enjoying tea at the back table was Pecora.

"I've been waiting for you. ♪"

Pecora had found me. She had found me spectacularly.

"He-he-he, I won't allow you to underestimate the demon king's power, he-he-he, he-he-he-he!"

Oh geez, she seems like she's having fun. Way too much fun.

On the other hand, my face was clouded over. She was definitely going to make me her toy...

Not even three seconds passed before Pecora stood and embraced me.

Oh whatever, do what you want. I'm almost used to it.

"Ohhh, I never knew my elder sister could be so adorable. I'm sure you're relatively powerless when you're this small, so I suppose I'll have to look after you for the rest of your life, won't I?"

I felt a chill. That side of her was the real peril...

"I wouldn't want to bother you for the rest of my life, so I would like to go back to normal..."

"Awww, what a waste! You should at least stay this way until I grow bored of it."

Those standards of yours make you a dangerous ruler! Don't draw the line at where you get bored!

"Indeed, let us ask your family."

A dark grin crossed Pecora's face. What a devil she was...

"Little Falfa, little Shalsha, do you think your mommy should stay this way? Or do you want her to go back to normal? You know, I'll send you as much candy as you want as long as she's like this."

"Oh no... What should I say...?"

"These options are extreme. It's like being confronted with the dilemma of *to be or not to be.*"

Gah! They're both being bribed with candy!

"Don't you want a little sister as cute as this?"

"Yeah, Falfa wants a little sister besides Shalsha! I want a little sister who's like a little sister!"

That was an awfully candid opinion, but I get it! Shalsha's not very little sister–like, at all.

"And Shalsha believes that by interacting with a younger sister, I will be educated in good taste."

Wait, wasn't it weird for the one getting the education in good taste to use the phrase *educated in good taste*? You wouldn't use that phrase if you weren't already educated!

"Falfa, Shalsha, please help your mommy! She wants to go back to normal!"

"Oh? Is your strategy to use tears to get your way, Elder Sister?"

"Pecora… Don't cheapen what I'm saying with your mudslinging…"

"I'm the demon king, though. ♪ Long ago, people considered me the embodiment of fear itself. ♪"

Pecora seemed to be having way too much fun. Well, the moment she'd discovered me, I knew things would turn out this way.

Fatla and Vania were also standing frozen in place, looks of guilt on their faces.

"All right, let's leave the jokes for now, and I'll suggest a way to restore my elder sister."

Phew. It sounded like she was going to actually cooperate.

"Thanks. I honestly thought you were going to lock me away…"

"I have a heart, you know," Pecora objected, puffing out her cheeks.

Then her demons-in-waiting spread out a cloth map before me.

"If it's detoxification you're after, then I think you should go to the apothecary at the very top of the World Tree. They say you can get any kind of medicine you want, from any era or any country. I'm certain you'll be able to remove whatever poison you need."

The World Tree, huh? It sure sounded like something straight out of a fantasy world, but I'd actually heard of it before.

That being said, its presence was legendary. That's because it was located in a land far away from where humans lived.

It was relatively far from Vanzeld Castle and the demon lands, even. The tree apparently sat in the middle of a huge forest.

"I guess we have no choice but to go all the way there."

"More haste, less speed. It's impossible that you get there and do not see improvements. It's much better than trying dubious recovery methods, is it not?"

When she said that, I had to give in.

For an example of what she was talking about, in medieval Europe, they did something called phlebotomies, or bloodletting, when someone was sick for a long time. They thought people would get healthy by taking out the bad blood. The point is, that didn't necessarily heal the body. In most cases, it would just weaken it.

"Fine. Then we'll head to this World Tree. Could you tell us a bit about its structure?"

"I could never refuse a request of my elder sister's."

According to Pecora's explanation, the inside of the tree was hollow—like a giant building, to put it simply.

She said that different races lived on the different floors. The demographic distribution was about 40 percent demons, 40 percent elves, and 20 percent dwarves.

"Then we just have to keep going up the building, right? Sounds easy enough."

"But the inside of the World Tree is like a very complicated maze, and they say only a few have reached the top floor. It's believed that would be the one hundred and eighth floor, even among the residents of the lower floors. There are plenty of areas along the way that are home to ferocious wild beasts."

Right, so it was like a big dungeon.

"That's fine. An adventure couldn't hurt once in a while."

My powers could probably find a way to take us to the top floor and get the antidote.

"Very well. We'll have Vania take you to the World Tree." Pecora smiled.

"Oh, I suppose I'll have to go... I'll do it anyway..." She didn't seem very happy about it...

"I'd be worried about my little sister on her own, so I'll go along." Fatla raised her hand. "And as a result of her neglecting her government duties, Lady Beelzebub is very busy and will not be able to join you."

"Ah, okay... I'm sorry about that."

Falfa seemed ready to announce she was coming along, but I just appreciated the sentiment.

"There's probably going to be dangerous spots if you two came along, so I want you to wait here, okay?"

"Indeed. I'm sure Beelzebub would be happy if the two stayed behind. ♪"

Pecora's imagination was gross, as was to be expected by now.

At the very least, I was just glad she wasn't coming along with us to the World Tree...

PERSE-
VERANCE
EQUALS
POWER. I
ONLY DO
THINGS I
CAN STICK
WITH!

AZUSA AIZAWA

The protagonist.
Commonly known
as "the Witch of
the Highlands."
A girl (?) who was
reincarnated as an
immortal witch with
the appearance of a
seventeen year old.
Before she knew what
was happening, she'd
become the strongest
being in the world.
Although she's had
some rough times, it
has ultimately given
her a family, and she's
delighted about it.

LAIKA

A dragon girl
and Azusa's
apprentice. She's
fastidious and cares
a lot about what
others think, but
she's a good, earnest,
hardworking girl.
Gothic Lolita clothes,
maid outfits, and
other frilly things suit
her very well (which
embarrasses her.)

LADY
AZUSA,
I'LL
DEVOTE
MYSELF
TO
IMPROVING
AGAIN
TODAY!

And so, the three of us—Vania, Fatla, and I—headed for the World Tree.

There were no problems with the flight there on Vania, but just as we were about to land soundly before the World Tree—

"It's such a shock to see it in person..."

That was my first impression of the tree stretching up and up toward the heavens. But still, its trunk was so thick that it almost seemed like an enormous wall.

I could see things that looked like branches and leaves above us, so I could just barely make out that it was a tree.

"It's been a long time since I've been to the World Tree. Not since my school trip," Fatla said with a straight face. It was probably a normal thing for her, but there was something strange about hearing a demon say *school trip*.

"We went to the same place on our school trip as you did, Fatla. We came here, too."

"I see, so you both came here on school trips. Then it seems like we'll get through this no problem, yeah?" I jogged lightly toward the entrance.

My stride was smaller now, so I had to jog or I'd fall behind.

Finally, I entered the World Tree.

However complicated and mysterious this dungeon may be, it's all to turn back to normal. I'll make it through this!

*　　*　　*

The moment I entered, I found this sign:

Elevator to the 10th Floor—just over there!
1 Adult: 1,300 koinne

"...Hey, what is this?"

And *koinne*, by the way, was the currency in the demon world. Nothing to do with koi fish.

"There are many people who keep wanting to go up and up the World Tree, so these elevators are a business. The farther up you go, the more money it costs, though," Fatla said, as though it wasn't a big deal at all.

"Wait, I heard that part of it was going to be like a dungeon, though..."

I could also see a sign that said WORLD TREE ORIGINAL MERCH over there. This reminded me way too much of the Skytree and Tokyo Tower and stuff...

"Some parts are. World Tree Eleventh Floor Wolves and World Tree Twelfth Floor Wolves inhabit the eleventh and twelfth floors respectively, so we must be careful."

"*Those* are the names people gave them?!"

"The World Tree Eleventh Floor Wolves are an endemic species that lives only on the eleventh floor of the World Tree. The World Tree Twelfth Floor Wolves are the same."

What a bizarre ecological system. Oh, Vania vanished while we weren't looking...

"Oh, sorry! I bought this at the shop over there!" Vania was holding a piece of fried bread that was covered in sugar. "They were selling World Tree Fried Bread over there, so I bought some. The fried bread here is so exquisite and very well-known!"

"You're just sightseeing at this point... Let me have a bite."

Sure enough, it was fried to perfection, and on top of that, the gritty sugar gave it a crunchy mouthfeel that was to die for. It was so good!

"I'll get one, too."

"You're small, so don't eat anything too greasy."

Fatla cautioned me, but I bought it anyway. *I probably won't be able to finish it all since I'm still the size of a kid... Oh well. I'll just munch on it bit by bit as we go.*

The elevator was manually operated by three burly Minotaurs pulling a string that hoisted the car upward, and in no time at all, we had arrived on the tenth floor.

And since I was a kid, I got in for half price. I was surprised they had the concept of child prices...

There were plenty of shops on the tenth floor as well and, for some reason, places serving food from the human world—it was like a food court.

"People who can't really fight only come up this far, you see. That's why there are so many restaurants," Vania said leisurely.

"There's a lot I could say about that, but let's head for the eleventh floor. We've still got a ways to go."

And so we headed for the eleventh floor, where wild creatures were said to dwell. At the stairs leading up to the eleventh floor, we had to donate to the Wild Animal Preservation Fund, so it cost us five hundred koinne each. But since I was considered a toddler, I didn't have to pay anything.

"By the way, there will be another tollgate on the way up to the thirteenth floor."

"Fatla, this business is raking it in, isn't it...?"

"It is. And incidentally, the farther up we go, the pricing incorporates transport costs so everything becomes more expensive. So please gather your supplies on the lower floors."

It was the rule of mountain sightseeing—drinks cost more the higher you went!

The eleventh floor was a thick, dark forest, making the sightseeing atmosphere of the previous floors seem almost deceptive.

Looking up, I saw there was a ceiling almost thirty feet above me. The walls of the World Tree's structure probably divided the floors as they were.

"It sure seems like a place to find frightening beasts."

I readied myself. *I'll fight as much as I need to!*

But that was all for nothing again.

A wolf approached me with a wheedling *awoooo*.

I tentatively patted it on its head, and it started wagging its tail happily.

"What the heck?! It's totally used to people! It's not wild at all!"

"The more powerful demons head for the higher floors, so they stopped fighting back at some point. I think they even have the habit of bowing their heads and asking for food."

Fatla had a World Tree guidebook open and was reading it.

I mean, it wasn't too strange to expect wolves to lose against demons…

"There will be no end to it if we start doting on them, so let us continue forward."

"It feels like all my expectations are being betrayed. Everything's upside down now…"

We got to the thirteenth floor and found another sign:

Elevator to the 17th floor—this way!
1 Adult: 2,200 koinne

"Not only is it more expensive but it doesn't even go that far…"

"Next, there will be creatures on the eighteenth floor. There is apparently the endemic species of the World Tree Eighteenth Floor Wildcat and the indigenous, valuable World Tree Eighteenth Floor Rose."

"And there'll be another even more expensive elevator, right?"

"According to the guidebook, the fare is three thousand koinne."

I finally understood the system. They were charging us for anything they could think of!

This whole business was devilish work! I knew the demons would think of something like this!

"This brings back memories! When we came on our school trip, I tried to see how far up I could get without spending any money, but I immediately got lost and then the sun went down and I missed the meeting time...!" Vania leisurely informed us.

"The residents here make a living off tourism, so they've purposely designed these mazes so they would be easy to get lost in. They install holes that are hard to jump through and add athletic obstacles. It's all a scheme to get you on an elevator," Fatla explained politely and bureaucratically. And still, what a stupid layout this was...

Afterward, we took many elevators, passed through plenty of wild areas, and finally managed to reach the thirty-eighth floor. It was about then that the sun started setting.

This floor was conspicuously lined with inns, like it was telling all those who were heading up to stay for the night.

I could see the view outside from my room at the inn. We were all the way up on the thirty-eighth floor, so it was a wonderful vista.

Not only that, but each room even had an outdoor bath overlooking the view.

"This is way different than how I imagined the World Tree to be."

Why was I, in my child's body, sitting in the bath, enjoying the view?

And the large tub was big enough for the three of us.

"The World Tree I imagined was a lone majestic-looking tree. Something with a more holy feel about it."

"The World Tree was once like that, apparently. However, it was unable to fight against the wave of tourism and ended up like this. Back then, there was an unprecedented boom in the sightseeing industry of the demon lands, so they built several inns and elevators."

Fatla was giving off an air of calm. Did she always feel like she was at work?

On the other hand, Vania was asleep in the bath. *Don't drown, okay?*

"It kind of feels like I'm looking at a miniature version of the world of my past life. There were plenty of places like this that became more and more touristy."

It seemed that the intelligent leviathan was thinking the same thing. "Well, there may be plenty of inns here on the thirty-eighth floor, but it will feel much like a real adventure soon. There are no more elevators after the eighth station."

That made it sound like we were climbing Mount Fuji…

"And, Miss Azusa, this might be a strange thing to say, but…" Fatla turned her gaze from the view outside to me. "I thank you for giving me this opportunity. It has been quite a long while since I traveled with my sister."

I was treated to a rare glimpse of their beautiful sisterly love.

"Oh yeah, you've been pretty busy with work, so you don't get to travel together much, do you?"

Traveling together was important for a family. *The girls and I should all go together somewhere sometime and take in some fresh air.*

"I'm sorry. This is also genuine work, however."

"Oh, it's fine. Sorry for dragging you along in all this nonsense."

I caught a flash of a smile on Fatla's face. *Aw, she's a good kid, too.*

"The floors above us will become smaller as well, so we'll ascend more quickly. Let us stay at the inn on the eighty-fourth floor tomorrow. There are no inns beyond that, and it will be like a true journey afterward."

"All right, we'll keep up a good pace."

We did indeed keep a good pace on our second day.

We pushed forward, our funds depleting with every step.

We stayed at an inn on the eighty-fourth floor, then made our way to our goal—the apothecary on the one hundred and eighth floor.

The beasts on the eighty-fifth floor and up were relatively dangerous and aggressively attacked us.

A sloth with an incredibly nasty look in its eye crawled along a tree growing inside the World Tree toward us.

"Whoa, it's coming right at us! Look at that drool streaming out of its mouth!"

"That's the Drooly Sloth."

Even though we had an enemy coming right for us, Fatla's eyes were still trained on the guidebook. There was no dignity in this nomenclature.

"What shall we do? Shall I protect you? You may use my sister as a shield, as well."

"Oh, no, that's okay." I closed the gap between the beast and me and sent the Drooly Sloth flying with a single punch. "Seems I'm still all right, stats-wise."

"Wooow, that was so cool!" Vania gave me an uninspired compliment.

And another creature was making its way over. It seemed like it was dashing right at her, scattering the grass around its feet.

"Ohhh, this is the Snotty Sloth. My older sister told me about this one."

"What's up with these animals?!"

Sure enough, something like snot was dripping from its nose. And it wasn't being slothful at all. It was running at full speed.

"Its snot has very high nutritional value that helps with the growth of the plants in the area. In return, the plants produce nuts and give them to the Snotty Sloth."

I hate this ecosystem...

"But it must want protein from animals as well, because it's attacking us, too. I suppose we should step out of the way, then."

Vania charged it and met it with a roundhouse kick.

A dull *thud* echoed throughout the floor.

The unconscious Snotty Sloth lay stretched out, twitching, and drool also started pouring from its mouth. *Gross.*

"Needless to say, we are strong, too. We're leviathans, after all."

I sometimes forgot I was surrounded by OP characters. Compared to the average inhabitant of this world, any one of them would be considered insanely strong.

"Indeed. My little sister won't slip up in a fight, either." Fatla seemed to have faith in her little sister when it came to this.

"Well then, let us hurry. If the shop closes, we will end up having to wait another day."

"That wouldn't be good. Falfa and Shalsha will probably be bored out of their minds."

"Oh, I don't think so. Our boss is probably happily looking after them. Actually, I'm sure she would rather us have our return be delayed!"

"That might be true, Vania, but you don't have to say it out loud!" Actually, I was more afraid of my two daughters getting too attached to Beelzebub.

We rushed forward without practically any rest.

We caught up to and passed plenty of other climbers (well, we weren't *literally* climbing, but we were in a way) who were headed to the top of the World Tree. Almost all of them were demons. We occasionally saw an elf or dwarf making the journey with demon escorts. They probably lived in the tree.

At around three in the afternoon, we finally came to the staircase leading up to the one hundred and eighth floor.

We finally, finally made it.

We all shared a look, nodded to one another, and slowly made our way up.

We opened the door at the top and exited to the outside of the World Tree.

The view was much more magnificent than what we'd seen in the hotels. Everything below looked like specks.

"Wow, we made it all this way. We made it! I'm so glad."

Unfortunately, I was too short, so the safety railings were in my way, and it was hard to see the whole view.

Then, Fatla lifted me up.

"I didn't say anything yet, though."

"I understand to a degree. We've come this far together, after all."

Ah, right. As we made our way to the top of the World Tree, a bond that tied our hearts together had been born among us.

Right beside us, Vania's voice had taken on a nasal tone. "Wait, what? I... This is odd... I'm not the type to cry... Ooh... But..."

Having finally arrived at the top floor, her tension had evaporated, and her heart was filled with an indescribable feeling. I knew, because I was experiencing the same.

"Stop. We're still at work," Fatla scolded, handing her younger sister a handkerchief.

But I could see she was trying to keep her composure.

I was sure it wasn't just because they'd been touched by the scenery.

For the first time in a very long while, the two sisters had overcome something together.

That was what this journey to the top of the World Tree was for.

"Let's rest for a sec. You can put me down."

I'll give the two some alone time right now.

"All right. Thank you."

Aw, she figured out that I'm giving them space. But it's no big deal if she knows, so I guess it's okay.

I sat down on a bench a short distance away from the sisters.

With their hands on the railing, the two of them spoke of the past. It sounded like they were talking about a time they climbed a volcano.

"If we were here when we were still kids, you would have jumped and almost fallen, Vania."

"I'm not that much of a birdbrain. You would have started complaining halfway through about how much of a chore this is, Big Sis. Then Dad would've said we shouldn't have taken you along in the first place."

"But I truly was tired when we climbed that volcano. It took so much longer than we planned."

"Not everything goes exactly according to schedule."

"You're just sloppy, that's all."

They both looked refreshed. *Aw, I'm jealous. I want sisters like that.*

It was a hassle coming all the way to the World Tree, but it was worth it. There were plenty of things I never would've seen if I'd stayed in the house in the highlands. So, so many.

Fatla and Vania finally came over to me.

"Both Vania and I have had enough of a break. You're ready now, aren't you?"

"Yeah. Let's go to the shop."

We were on the homestretch to the apothecary at the top floor—which wasn't more than a five-minute walk away around the outside of the tree.

There was a little plaza there. It was the perfect final spot for the World Tree.

More precisely, the tree continued farther up, and one could reach the top by taking the narrow staircase. We could do it to make our trip official, but I had to accomplish the goal in front of me.

There was a shop right next to the plaza. It was an apothecary stocked with all kinds of medicine.

I went inside and immediately found the lady elf working behind the counter.

Medicine lined the shelves. The place was almost like a department store for drugs.

"Excuse me—I ended up shrinking after eating some gnomesform, and I was wondering if there was any sort of treatment that would return my size to normal..."

I listed all my symptoms in great detail, and the employee nodded attentively. Judging by her expression, everything would be fine.

"In that case, we've recently learned that there is indeed a drug that is effective in curing these symptoms. I believe you'll be back to normal in no time!"

"Oh really! That's great news!" I patted my chest in relief.

"This medicine has been a big hit as of late, and we've learned that it cures your syndrome as well. That mushroom has been quite a pain to deal with in the past, so it's certainly a relief."

"Wow. What's it called, by the way?"

"This is it." The elf employee placed a bottle of medicine right in front of me.

Mandragora pills.

......

Now where have I heard that name before...?

In fact, it almost felt like I kept that *exact* medicine in my house as my go-to...

"You will feel better with this medicine, made by the famous Eno, the Witch of the Grotto! Ten pills should be enough to be effective. There are no poisonous ingredients, so that dose will be no problem!"

"Oh, uh, okay..."

I recalled the story of the bluebird of happiness. Who would've thought this whole mess could've been solved at home...?

The door opened, and the bell on it jingled. Someone had come in.

"Hello! It's me, Eno, Witch of the Grotto. I've brought three cases of your additional orders!" Eno stood holding some plain wooden crates.

"Why are you here, Eno?!"

"Hmm? Who is this little girl? ...Oh, it's the great Witch of the Highlands!"

Of course Eno would be shocked, too. I gave her a simple explanation of the poisonous mushroom. But to me, the real surprise was running into Eno here.

"Well, this apothecary is famous. Just having Mandragora pills on their shelves is a status symbol in itself. Ha-ha-ha! I've gotten so rich thanks to these. *So* rich! I'm thinking about redoing the grotto with a wine cellar and a billiards room. I cannot stop smiling!"

I think your character's changed. What happened to your social anxiety...?

"I mean, it's such a hassle to come all this way," I said. "It's so inefficient..."

"Huh? The shop has a transport wyvern that you can take to zip right to the top."

Wait, "zip right to the top"...?

"The World Tree apothecary has its entrance on the outside of the tree, so you can get here by wyvern. Dragons are a bit too big to fit, though."

So I ended up spending several days to get to a place I could've reached in a few seconds on a wyvern...? And the medicine was in my house all along...? Ugh... The fatigue is too much for this child's body...!

I slumped to my knees on the spot.

What the heck have I been doing...?

"Oh, great Witch of the Highlands, what's the matter?"

"I'm fine. I think it'll just take time to collect myself..."

Fatla and Vania appeared unable to speak at all. Judging by that, they didn't know we could've taken the wyvern to the top, either. It did sound like a kind of delivery route, so regular people probably didn't know about it.

It was like taking a really long stone staircase all the way up to a temple or shrine only to find out there was a route for cars in the back.

"What shall we do? I believe we have some Mandragora pills in the castle...," Fatla said apologetically.

"I may as well just buy them... It'll be like a memory of our trip."

I bought the Mandragora pills, made the return trip on Eno's wyvern, and arrived back on the ground.

Afterward, we rode on Fatla in her leviathan form back to the castle in silence.

"Aren't you going to take the medicine now?" Vania asked.

"I may as well just wait to take it and go back to normal in front of everyone."

"I see. That's a great idea!"

I was going to make good out of anything that came my way.

When we got back to the castle, Pecora said to us, "I'm so sorry, Elder Sister. I completely forgot that you can get there by wyvern. How careless of me."

"You definitely knew, didn't you...?" I could tell just by looking at her.

"Oh, it's no problem, is it? Walking around and climbing the World Tree is a fun experience on its own."

These things were totally unrelated, but now that we'd come this far, I wanted to go out with a bang.

"You should call over Beelzebub and my daughters now that I'm here. I want to turn into the old Witch of the Highlands in front of everyone."

"...Oh, that sounds interesting!"

There was a strange pause before she replied, but I couldn't see any problem.

And so Beelzebub, Falfa and Shalsha, my traveling companions Fatla and her sister Vania, and Pecora all gathered in Pecora's room.

"This whole thing has become quite an ordeal..." Beelzebub seemed apologetic, but it wasn't really anything for her to be sorry about. As the one who did the shrinking, it was my fault (and Halkara's for not checking thoroughly enough).

"It's fine. All's well that ends well. And now, I go back to being an adult!"

Falfa and Shalsha were also looking on with great interest.

Pecora still had that look on her face, and it bothered me a little...

"Here I go! Down the hatch, Mandragora pills!"

I swallowed ten pills with a cup full of water. All that was left was to get bigger.

And not all that much time passed before my body started to itch.

I see, so this is what growing feels like. Keep going; keep going!

The spectators also started making sounds of excitement.

But Shalsha still seemed dubious.

"Shalsha is apprehensive. When your body grows larger, those children's clothes won't stay on..."

"Ah—"

It was immediately followed by a feeling of extreme pressure, like my whole body was being squeezed in by a full-body cast...

©Benio

And then I heard a ripping sound.

My clothes were tearing all over the place! *Oh no!*

It wasn't like they were going to fly off me, but they were ripped enough that I couldn't show myself in public...

"Eeek! How shameless, Elder Sister! As your younger sister, I cannot watch this! Ahhh, eeep!" Pecora cried, all the while looking on with a delighted expression.

"Pecora, you knew this would happen, but you didn't say anything!"

"I am not quite sure what you're talking about. Absolutely no idea."

I couldn't believe I'd made this mistake... I think I was just plain panicking over shrinking... But still, I was surrounded by women I knew, so there wasn't too much harm in the end.

I crouched down in my tattered clothes and mumbled a plea to Beelzebub.

"Get me some clothes."

"Very well..."

But I wasn't going to let this go. "And after I get changed, we'll go to the big baths. All of us."

I had to come out on top somehow, so I decided we'd go to the baths again.

"It won't be that embarrassing if we all go to celebrate me getting back to normal, and—I'll see what you look like naked, Pecora! It's payback time!"

For some reason, Pecora's expression sobered. "Oh...Elder Sister, I'm not very used to that..."

For a second, I doubted her response, but it made more sense the more I thought about it. She was the demon king, so she probably never had much experience bathing with other people.

"Um... The most I ever dreamed of was a kiss, but anything more than that...was never written in books..."

I see... That was as far as her imagination went, then. This girl was more innocent than I thought...

I began to speak with a mischievous smile. I supposed I could get her back for what she did to me.

"Pecora, I'm telling you what to do as your elder sister. You will do exactly as I say or else."

Her face flushed, Pecora nodded.

The big baths at the castle really were big.

To put it simply, they were way bigger than any large-scale public baths I'd ever seen.

There were five baths in all. We decided to lounge around in the one that was scented with wine.

"Phew! Big baths are fantastic. They never get old."

We took a soak when we were climbing the World Tree as well, but it was much more worth it with more people.

"I agree. Work has tired me out so; the heat is spreading through me more than usual." Beelzebub liked hot springs to begin with, so she seemed very content.

The sister pairs of Falfa and Shalsha and Fatla and Vania pleasantly sat in the water.

But there was one demon king who seemed exceptionally embarrassed. She was soaking in another bath and wouldn't come to ours at all.

Pecora can't handle this.

I'd feel horrible ignoring her, especially because I was still acting as her elder sister, so I rushed to her side. We were close enough that I could instantly teleport with magic to her.

"Hello there."

"Eeep! How shameless, Elder Sister!"

We were in a bath—this wasn't shameless at all. You were *supposed* to wear nothing. You just weren't supposed to stare.

"You went a little too far with your jokes this time. All's well that ends well, since the two leviathans had a good time."

Pecora's eyes were swimming. Her whole personality had flipped.

"You really don't like bathing with everyone else, huh? Are you that embarrassed?"

"But everyone's breasts...are so big..."

Her gaze had dropped to my chest. *That's it...?* It wasn't like she would never see another girl's chest if she stayed alone the whole time... Would she faint if she saw Halkara's chest...?

I moved to sit right in front of her.

"Listen to me, Pecora. No matter what, I'm your elder sister. So when my little sister is bad, I scold her. Do you understand?"

Pecora nodded.

I thought about giving her a noogie, but I couldn't with her horns. Instead, I flicked her on the head. I was very careful of my power, of course.

"Um, I'm sorry..."

"Yes, very good. No hard feelings, now."

"Elder Sister, I have one request, though."

"Sure, hit me."

"Would you let me...touch your chest...?"

What...? What is she talking about...?

"I want to get more comfortable with this... I thought that per-haps...if I touched your chest, I might become impervious to it..."

"You may not!" I teleported back to my original bath in a hurry.

"Why not, Elder Sister?!" Pecora was running toward me.

"Because if you have any odd awakenings, then there's no going back! Plus, you're an authority figure, which makes things worse! What's gonna happen when you end up making dozens of demon girls cry?!"

This girl should stay innocent. For the sake of world peace.

"Elder Sister, please!"

"Your request is denied!"

I escaped from Pecora, thinking about how much hard work it was to be a big sister.

We recently placed a board in the dining room for sticking notes.

We had administrative notes, like whose turn it was to cook or clean, but there were also other things on it as well.

DAY 1:   25   ← *You can do more*

DAY 2:   23   ← *Moving around too much*

DAY 3:   26   ← *Steps are loud*

It kept going on and on after that, so I'll stop there, but the day with the number next to it was how many slimes Laika killed that day.

Over twenty was her general goal.

She apparently got motivation from looking at it. Keeping a record wasn't a bad thing at all.

I knew she could easily kill over a hundred in a day without breaking a sweat, even if they could be hard to find.

But I was the one who told her not to do that.

That's because if she couldn't do it without pushing herself, it would eventually become too difficult and leave her unable to do it at all.

That would just be putting the cart before the horse, so I was having her do enough each day that it became pure habit.

And the remarks beside the numbers were Flatorte pushing her onward. They were apparently killing slimes together. It didn't seem like they were really at odds, so I was letting them do as they pleased.

The two came back at around sunset that day. It was Laika's turn to cook dinner.

"We're back, Lady Azusa." "Mistress, we're home!"

The two greeted me as I sat at the table reading a book about especially valuable plants.

"Good work today, you two. Now go wash your hands, and be sure to gargle."

They went to the washing area that drew water from the well and came back. The house in the highlands was very civilized compared to the rest of the world.

Even after Laika went to the kitchen, she did some practice swings—more like practice punches. Cute as she was, she was a dragon, so one of those hits would kill a normal person. It would be like getting clocked by a pro martial artist who was throwing a serious punch.

"Your movements are much sharper than they used to be. I don't know if there's much point in practicing in human form, though…"

"Do you think so? I'm so glad! And there is a point; no matter what form I am in, my perception is the same as it is when I am a dragon."

Then she could continue training to be the strongest.

"Perseverance is power. I will become the strongest dragon!"

I wasn't very preoccupied with strength, so I had no idea what could come of being the strongest dragon, but it was probably like an athlete aiming for even greater heights.

That was the kind of thing you called competing with yourself. It was always good to try to improve yourself, no matter what it was. As long as you didn't stray into the realm of overwork.

While I pondered that, Laika called out as she opened and closed all the cupboard doors.

"What? We don't have any carrots or onions."

Uh-oh. That wasn't like missing herbs for some extra flavor. Those were key ingredients.

"Oh right, Falfa and Shalsha went out for shopping and haven't come back yet. I wonder if they got sidetracked…"

They were both diligent kids, so I doubted they would give up halfway through their shopping. *Oh no—maybe they're so cute that they got kidnapped…?! All because they were too cute… I guess it's possible…*

As that thought crossed my mind, the two came home.

"Sorry we're laaate."

"Something caught our eye, so we went on a hunt."

They each carried one pack of woven wood, both stuffed to the brim.

Looks like they did bring home some vegetables.

"You *are* late. Hurry up and give the veggies to Laika. She won't have anything to cook with."

"Big Sis Laika, I'm sorry." "My apologies."

The two apologized to Laika as they handed their shopping over to her. They were just in time.

But I was interested in Shalsha's comment. Indeed, not only were they late, but they had a reason.

"Hey, Shalsha, what was it that caught your eye?"

For better or for worse, very little ever changed in Flatta. *Idyllic* was the perfect word to describe it.

"There was a poster on the announcement board saying a famous minstrel had come to the village."

"A minstrel? Didn't know that."

There were generally two types of minstrels: ones who were invited to various royal courts (and eventually became court musicians) and drifting artists.

If one had come to Flatta, then it was very likely they were the wandering type. Some of them were still well-known, so it made me wonder.

"Falfa helped Shalsha search the village. But we couldn't find anything."

"All our effort was wasted."

So that's why they were late coming home. That made sense.

I glanced at the calendar. Luckily, I had tomorrow off. Halkara didn't have work that day, either.

Which meant the minstrel's plan was probably to perform on the holiday.

"Now you've got Mommy interested, too. All right, tomorrow, we'll go looking for this minstrel."

Shalsha nodded eagerly, and Falfa jumped up with a "Yay!" Their reactions were so different.

But by the ceiling above us, Rosalie wore a dubious look.

"I know quite a bit about renowned minstrels, you know. They used a square near the building I once lived in as the town's performance venue, so I caught a lot of shows."

"I see. You've been watching the wandering minstrels for a long time, then."

"Has there been anyone recently who would come all the way out here because they're famous? There's Mohawk Santol, I guess. Or maybe Raikkonen the Phoenix…? But they wouldn't come out to Flatta…"

I didn't know much about the music industry here, but there had to be someone. Probably.

The following day, the family left the house in the morning for Flatta.

And sure enough, there was a garish-looking poster hanging on the bulletin board outside the town.

*　　*　　*

WORLD-FAMOUS MINSTREL

SCHiFANoiA

FIRST-EVER TOUR TO FLATTA!

Her lute growls!
Her lute wails!
Lose yourself in SOULFUL VOCALS!
Drown in her masterful
performance and
ingenious lyrical world!

*Tips are very much appreciated. Thank you.

"What the heck is this…?"

This was *not* the kind of minstrel I was imagining…

It looked like an ad for a rock concert…

"Hey, Rosalie, do you know this Schifanoia?"

"They're probably no one. I've never heard of them."

Something smelled really fishy about all this. Yet another weirdo had come by.

My gut was telling me we'd probably be better off staying away from them. Trouble always seemed to find me.

"This is different from the minstrels I know," said Laika. "Long ago, when I used to visit human towns, I would go into the town halls to listen to their performances. I almost never listened to the wandering minstrels performing in the streets."

I guess it was like people in Japan who only ever listened to musicians who'd debuted professionally.

"Judging by what Laika said, I guess there are some odd ducks among wandering minstrels. I'm positive we shouldn't—"

"Wooow! What songs are they gonna sing? Falfa wants to know!"

"Shalsha did want to see it in person at least once."

Oh, great! My daughters are way into this!

"Hey, you two, I'm sure there are other things that would be much more interesting... Oh, maybe we should go to Nascúte for the day?"

"Falfa wants to see the minstrel."

"The poster was written by someone very confident, and it could be fun to give them a listen at least once."

Crap! Should I just drag them somewhere else, then? But that wouldn't be fair to my daughters...

Flatorte had been silent the entire time as I struggled with some minor inner conflict.

I started to think maybe she wasn't very interested, but something felt different about her.

"Schifanoia, huh? She's been around for ages. Could call her a veteran, even."

"Wait, you actually know her?!"

"I am obsessed with minstrels. I believe I know over a thousand groups."

So *that's* where she was putting all her energy.

"A thousand...? And here I was, pretending like I knew anything about minstrels. Now I'm just embarrassed..."

Rosalie, who'd declared that Schifanoia was a nobody, looked like she wanted to disappear. She'd probably crawl into a hole if there was one nearby—but she was a ghost, so she could hide in a wall or a rock even if there wasn't. But I wouldn't want her to get stuck like last time.

"There are types of minstrels who travel to every little town and village by foot, and others who only change venue within larger cities and never bother to travel to places with smaller populations."

To put Flatorte's explanation in terms of Japan, some rock bands traveled all throughout the country, but there were also bands that only ever performed in Tokyo.

"Schifanoia was the type to perform every once in a while in the royal capital, but she's suddenly started a worldwide tour. I'm not surprised Rosalie doesn't know about her."

I'll trust the word of the great critic, Professor Flatorte. It wouldn't be a waste of time to go check out an artist who a family member was familiar with.

"All righty, then, let's go find this minstrel Schifanoia!"

"Okaaay!" "Understood."

Falfa and Shalsha almost immediately dashed into the village.

We spotted a woman in the town square holding an instrument resembling a lute.

Except it was less of a lute and more of a guitar. The angular design reminded me of an electric guitar.

Long rabbit ears stuck out from the top of her head—she was part of an animal race called the almiraj. You could spot those ears from a distance. That and the puff-ball tail were the unique characteristics of the almiraj.

The rest of her looked like a regular human girl, but almiraj were also considerably long-lived.

Everything about her outfit was aggressive.

Her skirt was really short, and she wore spiked bands around her arms and neck.

There wasn't much in the way of entertainment in the village, so there were about thirty people gathered around her. It looked like the concert was just about to start.

The almiraj strummed her lute and began to sing.

"WOOOOOOOOAAAAAAAAH, DEJTRUCTION, DEJTRUCTION, DEJTRUCTION! WOOOOAAAAAAAAHHHHHH, EXECUTION, EXECUTION, EXECUTION! THE JUUUN, AAAAAAAAAAAND THE MOOOOOOOOOOOON, JTART TO DAAAAAAAAAAAAAA AAAAAAAAAAAAAAAAAAAANCE! HELL AND HADEJ AND THE UUUNDERWOOOOOOOOOORLD!"

After about fifteen seconds, I knew I was right.

We shouldn't have come!

It was kind of fun to watch her ears bouncing back and forth when she was headbanging during her guitar solo (look, it was more guitar than lute, so I'm calling it a guitar), but I didn't really understand this kind of musicality...

I guess it was generally the style to scream something. She was playing the lute well, but her voice was too loud. I think she should've just played the lute without any singing...

"My old ears are ringing." "Let's go home, Grandpa." "Daddy, can I have butter candy?" "Let's play chess over there."

Oh, the audience around her was gradually disappearing.

"Waaahhh! I'm scared!" "Let's go, Big Sis."

Falfa started crying, and so Shalsha took her away...

I knew I should've stopped them. I'm their mother, after all...

Laika, Halkara, and Rosalie were all looking on, dumbfounded.

It was true that I wasn't sure how to interpret this.

When the first song was finished, the only ones left in the audience were pretty much just my family (minus two). Everyone else had been waiting for the song to be over to go home.

But in the middle of it all was Flatorte, standing with her arms crossed and listening intently.

"Hmm, that was a very Schifanoia-esque song. I knew it was her within the first five seconds or so."

She was talking about something...

"You knew that song?"

"Mistress, of all the itinerant minstrels, Schifanoia is considered to be more of the death style within the crime subdivision of the emotional style. This is a very typical death-style song. That being said, Schifanoia leans more toward isolation style within the death genre. Isolation-leaning involution style, you could say."

There are too many subgenres!

"Ha-ha-ha! Is my glorious voice tearing y'all up?!"

Oh no! Schifanoia was starting to MC. Now it was even harder to leave...

"This is my first time here in Flatta on tour, but I can feel the energy!"

Hold on. Literally nobody was clapping even after the first song!

"This is the countryside, so this glorious set list is comprised of my most famous songs. This next one is my signature song, 'Gray Dreams'!"

It might be her signature song, but I'd obviously never heard of it!

"BLACK AND WHIIIIIIIIIIIIIIIIIIIIIIIIIIIIIITE, WOOOOOOO OOOOOOAAAAAAAAAAH! AAAAAAAAAAAHHHHHHHHHH! PUT THEM TOGETHEEEEEEEEEEEEEEEEEEERRRRRRRRRR, YOU GET GRAAAAAAAAAAAAAAAAAAAAAAAAAAAAY! ADD MORE BLAAAAAAAAAAAAAAAAAAAAAAAAAAAAACK, MAKES IT GRAYEEEEEEEEEEEEEEEEEEEEEEEEEER!!"

Sloppy lyrics. Needed to have a little more of a message.

Flatorte still stood with her arms crossed and occasionally nodded.

"Ahhh, this is an over-the-top involution style. I'm surprised this is enough to whip up her audience."

"Sorry, I don't understand a thing you said."

"See, crime style places the lute front and center over the vocals, but death style, especially, creates an earsplitting sound. And isolation style, as its name suggests, tends to have passionate lyrics about loneliness and isolation, and involution creates the feeling of the performer and audience becoming one during the live performance."

I got the impression that she was talking the entire time about a magical system I knew nothing about.

Laika tapped me on the shoulder. "Excuse me, but Miss Halkara is not feeling well, so I am going. And Miss Rosalie said she's not interested, so she's leaving, too."

"Oh, okay, sure..."

"My heel is very itchy in my shoe," Halkara said, "but I can't seem to scratch it, so I need to leave." *Okay, I understand that having an itch you can't scratch is tough, but that's not even a fake illness.*

Maybe I should've said that we were leaving… But I couldn't find the heart to say that I was going, too. Flatorte was listening, after all.

The second song soon ended.

"Well! Looks like my glorious power left some people so breathless, they had to leave!"

And she kept calling everything "glorious."

"Our third song will be 'Drownin' in the Moon,' which makes the crowds go wild in the capital!" she said as she started tuning her strings. It looked like this was going to take a while.

A few things were bothering me, so I took the opportunity to ask Flatorte my questions.

"Are people in the capital really into this stuff?"

"Well, minstrels like Schifanoia will draw audiences of about thirty."

"That's…not a lot…"

It's not like no one was listening to her, but I couldn't say the number was high.

"Of those thirty, I believe about fifteen would be fellow minstrels in the same industry."

That's half!

"Of course, those kinds of numbers won't pay the bills, so I think Schifanoia makes ends meet with money from a part-time job."

She was just a crappy one-woman band…

"How many crazy fans are there who know all these minstrels like you do…?"

"Actually, I'm just one of many all over the country. I'd say most live in the capital, since many minstrels are only active there."

"If you can pick out Schifanoia, does that mean she's good?"

"She's lower-middle. There are plenty of other minstrels with more skill. Her worldview is conventional, and she lacks originality." Flatorte was quick to shut her down.

"Then why are you listening to her, Flatorte? She's not that good, right?"

A bitter smile crossed Flatorte's face. She must have gotten that question a lot.

"I don't only listen to good musicians. I will listen to anyone, so long as they're a minstrel. That's part and parcel of being a minstrel fan."

Words of one who was in way too deep.

I'd never been such a serious fan about anything, so I didn't really understand.

"Actually, even if they are over-the-top or just bad, I find myself getting more excited the more extreme or terrible they are."

"Yeah, I don't know about that..."

I remembered the people who would perform on the street at night when I was a corporate slave.

Sometimes they'd be playing and talking the whole time while only one or two people listened...

That made it really awkward to stop and listen, so I always just passed straight by, but there *were* people who would take time to listen. Flatorte was one of them.

It looked like Flatorte was listening, so I figured it was a good time to excuse myself.

It was so painful to stay in this climate, and I wasn't even interested.

—And then the minstrel lifted her head and met my eyes.

"I'm so thankful I have so many believers out here in the country-side! Two...two thousand! Glorious!"

She multiplied us by a thousand! And she's totally recognized me as a fan... I can't leave now!

"I can hear your screams!"

You're the only one talking!

"And we'll go straight into the fourth song after this!"

Crap! Timing my escape is getting more and more difficult!

Afterward, there was a string of songs that employed a technique Flatorte called "lute shredding," and Schifanoia was screaming almost all the lyrics, so I had no idea which song was which. What song were we on now...?

"THE CLOOOOOOOOOOOOOWN SMIIIIIIIIIIIIIIIIIILES AT NIIIIIIIIIIIIIGHT! WOOOOOOAAAAAAAAAAH!"

I stood there blankly, but it looked like the performer was hard at work. She was dripping with sweat, exhausted.

"Bwa-ha-ha-ha... You finally caught up to me... So I guess now I'll explain our glorious merch... Here we have the Schifanoia original towel for one thousand gold... It's very absorbent, so it's great when you're as gloriously sweaty as I am..."

It was time for some announcements.

The towel, by the way, had a cute bunny pattern on it. I wouldn't mind one.

I completely missed my timing to run for the hills, though. At least it sounded like the concert was going to be done soon.

"N-now... It's time for the last song... 'Necromancy'... Urgh, I—"

With that, she collapsed.

The song was called "Necromancy," so maybe she was going to perform a dead body coming back to life. That was pretty complex.

......

Twenty seconds passed but still nothing. This would be a broadcast disaster if she was on TV or the radio.

......*Hmm?*

Could she *really* have collapsed?!

"Mistress, this is bad! Schifanoia has lost consciousness!"

"I knew it! We have to help her!"

If this was a proper live concert, then she would have tour staff, but this was definitely a solo gig. Her whole audience of two had to take care of her.

This wasn't peaceful at all.

It was because in my past life, I'd collapsed and died of overwork. This was too much like my own situation for me to look the other way.

I approached her and cast some recovery magic on her.

This typically would solve everything, though. But even when the color came back to her face, her pained expression didn't change. Could she have a terrible illness…?

"Th-thanks… To think one of my believers would save me… This is the greatest blunder of my glorious life…"

Phew. She was conscious again.

"Um, I know that might be your stage persona, but you can act normally now. Is there anything wrong? Please tell me!"

"M-my glo—"

"If that 'glorious' thing is an act, then please stop it."

Schifanoia didn't say anything for a little while. "My…health is fine… In all my eighty years as an almiraj, I've never gotten sick…"

I knew she'd talk normally once she quit acting.

"I'm hungry… I have almost no money while I'm on tour, so I haven't eaten all that much…"

"I see. I get it. I think I've got a grasp on the situation now."

Her body was weirdly light. Way too light, in fact.

It would be no trouble to carry her to a doctor and have them solve this. She'd definitely been pushing herself all this time; I could look after her for a bit. Flatorte knew a lot about the industry, and she was already here.

"Flatorte, get Laika and the others. We'll take her home and fatten her up."

"Are you sure, Mistress? You seemed like you couldn't be bothered before."

"We've come too far to turn back. I collapsed like this once. This is probably a chronic problem, so I want to solve it the right way."

There wasn't much I could do if the minstrel herself refused, though.

"Thank you… My real name is Kuku…"

It didn't seem like she was going to run away.

And her real name was much cuter than her stage name…

"Would it be bad for your schedule if you canceled your concerts?"

"I did not announce my dates beforehand, so it's all right."

She really was going freestyle.

I assembled my family, told them the situation, and took Kuku to the house in the highlands.

Laika cooked food and brought it over, but the plate was empty in the blink of an eye.

She was like a bear right before hibernating who had to eat everything in sight at any chance she got.

"It's so good! It's so good!"

She tore into the food like she'd been on the brink of starvation, and Halkara and Flatorte watched on with mouths agape. "It is all worth cooking to have someone eat so happily!" Laika said. That was reasonable.

The more food filled her stomach, the more color came back to Kuku's face.

It was like I was watching a game where the recovery items were cooked food. Like your life gauge filling up the second you ate a pizza. When I played a long time ago, my child's mind thought the character's body was weirdly constructed to recover right after eating.

In the end, Kuku scarfed down enough food for about five people. Afterward, I let her use the bath.

After she got rid of her heavy eye makeup, she looked like a frail and timid girl with bunny ears.

Once Kuku finally caught her breath, we decided to talk.

I sat her down with Flatorte, who was extremely knowledgeable about wandering minstrels, and Rosalie, who knew some things about them.

"I know it's none of my business, but you're not living a sustainable lifestyle, are you? Have you collapsed like that in the past?" I asked her, and she suddenly acted like she was being interrogated.

She didn't seem to be the very sociable type.

She had been so concentrated on eating, she must not have paid much attention to us until now.

"I have…collapsed in the past… Several times…"

Her voice was relatively quiet, which made her sound sweet. It was totally different from when she was yelling and glorious-ing everything.

"Being a minstrel isn't enough to feed me, so I work a lot of part-time jobs… Most of them late at night so they don't conflict with my music… And so sometimes I'm sleep-deprived…"

"Ahhh, I get it now."

Some people pushed themselves too far in pursuit of their dreams.

"I thought I would get more tips on my on-foot tour this time… And…there are many days where I don't even get a single gold… I've done my best to make my food budget last…"

Of course she would collapse. I almost got the impression that she was even working *to* collapse.

"They do say that there is a small percent of wandering minstrels who make good money. Of the ones known to me, Flatorte, there's Pilot Fish and Andersen and Snow White and the Cold Black Tea Group…"

I didn't know any of the names that Flatorte listed, but I did get that it was a tough business.

"But those kinds of minstrels gather an unbelievable amount of money. I have heard that they can make three million gold in one day."

"Three million in one day… Theoretically, one day of work could feed me for a year," Kuku commented with a murmur. "I've…always wanted to be like them, too… I left the almiraj village sixty-three years ago… I said I'd become a big minstrel one day…that I'd become a great death-style minstrel, that I'd throw away my weak self and live the death lifestyle…"

Just like a kid leaving their home to go to Tokyo to become a famous artist. She must have chosen that character for herself because her own personality was timid as well.

"But—" Kuku cut herself off.

A teardrop hit the table. She was crying.

"I-I've remained totally obscure… No one comes to watch me… I've thought about quitting so many times, but I always tell myself, just one more year…"

Ahhhhh! Just listening to her was making *me* sad! Knowing when to throw in the towel definitely isn't easy...

"Waaaaaaaahhh! What a sad story!"

Rosalie was bawling!

Tears were streaming down her face. Her ghost tears weren't corporeal, though, so nothing got wet.

"You've been through so much! I completely understand. Minstrels who came to Nascúte were like that, too, and so many of them struggled to put on a smile!"

Rosalie had seen much of the world, so she could sympathize.

I could understand Kuku's story to some extent. I didn't have any personal experience, but my friend's little brother had gone to Tokyo to be an actor. Luck hadn't been on his side, and he hadn't done all that well. He'd said half of his income was from part-time work...

It wasn't at all unusual for someone who periodically appeared in movies and dramas to barely make ends meet, and it was apparently very tough to become famous doing that.

"You were undernourished enough that you collapsed, so you can stay and relax here for a while."

Kuku looked shocked, but her face clouded. It seemed forced.

"I'm glad. But, um..."

"But?"

"I-I'll have to get the okay from my agency...I think, so..."

"You have an agency?"

Something was fishy here.

"Mistress, Schifanoia has never been a part of any agency. She's an independent artist," Flatorte, the minstrel nerd, informed me.

"I-I'm sorry... That was a bluff... I wanted to sound cool..."

Why was she trying to put on a cool front *now*? Well, everyone had a line they wouldn't cross for the sake of their pride, so that was probably it.

"Stay here for at least five days to get your strength back. We're in the highlands, so the air is fresh. It's not a bad place to recuperate."

"Yes, Mistress! How good of you! So generous!"

I thought Flatorte wanted to praise me, but it sounded like she was making fun of me…

Rosalie stood before Kuku. Floated—not technically standing.

"Then I'll show ya to an empty room. I'm sure you'll be ready to jump back into those creative endeavors, too. Pump out those new songs!"

Kuku responded with a miserable half smile, but her expression turned downcast. "Thank you, but, um… I've been thinking that it might be time to stop my music career… That it might be time to break up Schifanoia…"

"You're breaking up even though you work alone?" Flatorte pointed out.

"That's… I'm sorry; I was acting again…"

This girl had a tendency to be self-conscious when it came to stuff like this.

"I was thinking that it might be time to punctuate Schifanoia's long career and announce a final act… And then maybe start walking a new path…"

It sounded like she was being dramatic again, but I knew what she wanted to say. Everything came to an end eventually. That wasn't a bad thing in and of itself. It was her own choice. She could stop today or in ten years. She didn't need anyone's permission.

But when I saw Kuku's expression, something caught my attention.

"Hey, Kuku, do you have any plans or dreams for your next life?" I asked outright.

"I'm going to buy a lottery ticket, win the hundred-million-gold prize, and spend the rest of my life lazing around—that is my first choice."

"I don't want your jokes. Answer honestly."

She was taking life more lightly than I thought, so I was a little irritated.

"You're right… I'm sure if I keep working part-time…I think I might find out who I really am…"

"I didn't expect much, but you *really* have no idea, do you?!"

Even if this girl took a break from the music life, she didn't have a plan for afterward.

"Well, Mistress, even if she continued acting as Schifanoia, she wouldn't make any money, so as a result, she would be better off working more hours part-time than she is now."

"Flatorte, those scathing comments just come to you as naturally as anything, and you're not even being sarcastic."

Not that I could exactly offer her any empty encouragement about how continuing her music would bring her lots of money.

But then Kuku's face flushed red, and she pressed her right hand against her mouth. After all this time, I couldn't imagine that her real character was hopeless, too.

"A-actually...I've received plenty of offers like these in the capital city..."

Kuku placed several pamphlet-looking things on the table.

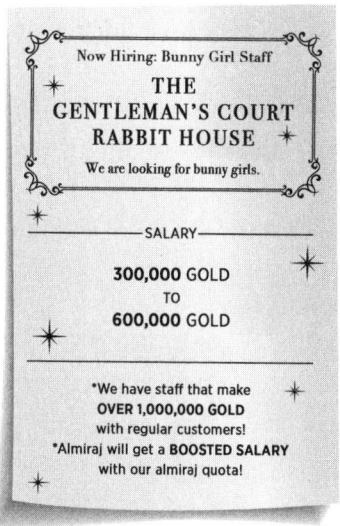

Now Hiring: Bunny Girl Staff

THE GENTLEMAN'S COURT RABBIT HOUSE

We are looking for bunny girls.

———— SALARY ————

300,000 GOLD
TO
600,000 GOLD

*We have staff that make **OVER 1,000,000 GOLD** with regular customers!
*Almiraj will get a **BOOSTED SALARY** with our almiraj quota!

A wholesome café with only animal waiters

Fun Animals

———— SALARY ————

500,000 GOLD
TO
800,000 GOLD

For more information, please visit the shop in the first-floor basement of the building next to the Woodpecker Village bar in the East 8th District.

"..."

There were others, but most of them were like this.

They were all extremely sketchy.

"Oh, animal races are in high demand for such jobs... I, Flatorte, was once scouted when I was walking around the capital. 'You think I would work at such a low-brow shop?' I said. 'How dare you mock a blue dragon!' Then I gave them a taste of my ice breath for good measure."

You can't just breathe ice on people. But I know how you feel.

"Almiraj are especially popular. To make matters worse, such establishments even make use of what they call 'bunny girl' outfits. I'm not surprised that Schifanoia was scouted."

Actually, I was surprised to learn there were bunny girls in this world. But since this was a world of humans with horns and animal ears, such things would probably seem normal to anyone else.

"I'm often told that I can make a lot of money in this industry and that I'm a good fit, since I will look young for a long time..." Kuku dropped her shoulders with a fragile smile. "I always turned them down at first because I was confident I would keep going with my music, but I haven't gotten anywhere after all this time. Maybe I should just work for people who ask me to..."

Wait, all occupations might be equally honorable, but this would not do.

"Well, let me ask you one thing. Are you okay with this, Kuku? Are you not interested in music anymore?"

Kuku immediately shook her head. I could see more willpower in her eyes than there had been earlier.

"Of course I'm not okay with it! I love music!"

"Well, then you don't need to waffle on anything at all."

I nodded vigorously.

"You shouldn't quit music. You need to keep going!"

I declared it with confidence.

"You might not be making any money as a minstrel right now. But you must love it to some degree; otherwise, you wouldn't have been doing it for as long as you have. To just put a lid on it and lock it up inside you—I think you'd regret that someday."

People often got absorbed in things when they were young.

That was why they sometimes got bored of it and ended up interested in something else.

But the artist Schifanoia wasn't someone who'd finished her career after such a short time. She loved it so much for how bad she was at it, but in a way that made her and music complement each other well.

I lifted myself a little out of my chair to lean forward and grasp Kuku's hand.

"Ah, um…"

I caught her by surprise.

But I had to show her that my feelings ran deep. Otherwise she might view me as a complete stranger offering advice from the comfort of my own home.

"I wouldn't stop you if you were to look ahead for different work. But you're facing backward, moving on because you think you have no other choice. And that's why you need to keep working!"

I'd lived in Tokyo in my past life, so I saw and heard plenty of people with shattered dreams who went back home.

Most of them wore bitter smiles to try and trick themselves into believing they didn't mind.

Their true feelings, *I'm not okay with this*, were written all over their faces. But whether they wanted to or not, they would sometimes have to go back for familial or financial reasons.

But people still had to make up their minds. No one could live out all possibilities at once. That was why I held those decisions in high regard.

But Kuku hadn't made up her mind—she'd chosen a path other than music by process of elimination.

I had to stop that.

"First, you need to think long and hard about music. If the problem is that you're not selling, then think about that. You can stay as long as you need to until then! You'll be fed three times a day! And then, when you decide what to do about your future, you can go back to the capital!"

"Wah… Are you sure…? I don't think I can pay rent…"

"Don't worry about that. I'm the one who told you to keep making music, so I'll keep up with you however I can! I want you to go back to the capital with pride!"

I might've decided too much on my own, but I couldn't just wave her off and wish her good luck back home.

"Our mistress is our mistress, isn't she?"

"Big Sis is Big Sis. Yep, I knew it!"

Flatorte and Rosalie sounded like they were giving their approval or something. I thought what I was doing was pretty natural, though…

And so, that was how we temporarily gained another family member in the house.

"I'm Kuku the almiraj… It's nice to meet you…"

Kuku introduced herself to the rest of the family that night. She must have been wondering what sort of relationship my family had. Thinking about it rationally, we were an odd bunch.

"There aren't any houses around here, so you can play the lute at night, too. You can play as much as you want until my daughters' bedtime."

"O-okay… To commemorate our newfound relationship, I'll perform a bit…"

Kuku stood before everyone, lute in hand.

She spun around then faced us again.

When she did, her expression was way different from the meek one she had just been wearing.

Wait, she's changed character?!

"WAH-HA-HA! WELCOME TO THE BANQUET OF GLORIOUS DEATH AND DESTRUCTION! AND NOW, THE FIRST SONG! POISON POISON POISON, POISON POISON, POISON POISON POISON POISON, POISON POISOOOOOOOOOOOOOOOOOOOOOOOOOOOOON!"

Oh, she changed into her Schifanoia persona!

There was a deafening metallic scream coming from her lute.

"ABƧIIIIINTHE, ABƧIIIIIIIIIIIIIIIIIIIIIIIIIIIINTHE!"

But, as always, her lyrics were a mystery to me.

Falfa wasn't a fan, as she covered her ears with her hands, and her eyes were squeezed shut like (> <). It didn't suit her at all.

Shalsha was Falfa's complete opposite, in her own way, sound asleep in a chair. *Seriously? You can sleep with noise like this? Wait, it's supposed to be music, so I suppose it'd be rude to call it noise.*

The elegant Laika had her head tilted, and Halkara seemed bored.

Either way, I could tell by their reactions that they weren't liking it very much.

Rosalie really was relatively hardy, so she was listening with some interest.

"She's not wearing any makeup right now, so the impact is a little weak. Maybe she should spike all her hair straight up?"

You want to make this more extreme…?

And of course, Flatorte was the unique one of the family. She stood with her arms crossed, as though she was making sure of something.

"I see. This first song is 'The Era of Poison (Demon Year 28 Version).'"

"What are demon years, Flatorte?"

"Schifanoia has created her own calendar called the Demon Calendar to represent the years she's been active. In essence, that means that was an arrangement she wrote in her twenty-eighth year after debuting. The original song, 'The Era of Poison,' is from the year after she debuted and is the classic example of her early work. The first time she performed was at a bar in the capital called Life Is a Dream, attracting an audience of sixteen."

Wow, Flatorte really knew a lot. Too much, actually. And it would've been nicer to have a bigger audience…

As we chatted, the song ended.

"Wah-ha-ha-ha-ha! I'm gloriously pumped up now! Our second song is 'The Flower Blooming on the Execution Grounds'!"

"I see—she's including headbangers as well."

"Where are you getting this information, Flatorte? You don't even bang your head."

"I, Flatorte, am the kind who simply wants to listen to music. I will not go wild. It's dangerous for a blue dragon to lose control."

The reason was more realistic than I thought. Even though she was in human form now, it sure would be a big problem if she got so worked up by the music that she transformed back into a dragon...

"All riiiiiight! Next, we'll go straight through 'A Million Years at War,' 'The Bloody Saint,' and 'The Crow's Sins' all at once!"

Ohhh, this was bad. This was going to take more time than I thought. She wasn't going to stop after just one or two songs.

"Waaah! I can't tell the difference among the songs! They all sound the same!"

Falfa, your criticism is way too honest for this! Keep it to yourself!

"Sorry, Kuku. Do you think you could stop now?"

More than half of the people here didn't want to listen, so it was probably best to stop this.

"Wh-who are you talking about? M-my name's Schifanoia! I don't have such a cute name! I'm here to deliver you true, glorious despa—"

"Yeah, you don't have to do that anymore."

"...Okay, I understand... I'm sorry." She was Kuku again. "It was such a sudden performance that I don't think I played very well... I think I messed up on my lute twice..."

"I don't think that's the problem."

By all appearances, we would need more time to solve this than I thought...

There wasn't much point in asking the opinions of the family members who weren't interested in music, and they probably wouldn't know what to say anyway. Thus, I had Flatorte do the coaching.

We moved to Flatorte's room and started our review session. I joined in, too, as the one who'd decided to let her stay here. It would be odd if I acted like an outsider.

"First, let me just say this from the listener's perspective—isolationist death style isn't popular in this day and age. It's not a good choice because it's not attracting any listeners."

"Y-you're right..." When she was Kuku, this girl was honest and kind of negative, so she readily accepted what Flatorte had to say.

So it was the genre that wasn't catching on after all.

"Why don't you change Schifanoia's music to the floral subgenre of overkill style? I mean, it's extremely compatible with crime style, don't you think?"

There she goes again with jargon I don't know! The minstrel industry is too complicated!

"I—I...am going to stay within the crime genre... Actually, I'm proud that I'm different from the overkill artists... Even though it is popular..."

Oh no. I'm glad I came, but I don't understand anything at all, so I have nothing to contribute.

"I know what you want to say, Schifanoia. I am questioning the recent trend in the minstrel scene that only values overkill. But it wouldn't be bad to incorporate the good elements. Like the crime-style minstrels the Church of Holy Tears—they switched to overkill and were a big hit."

"I understand, but...I prefer to prove myself as a skilled death artist..."

It seemed creators who were insistent on their ways existed in every world.

"Hmm. Schifanoia, you're afraid of creating a hit, aren't you?"

Flatorte's eyes were cool as she spoke.

"Th-that's not it... That's not true at all... I just have an attachment to death style since it emphasizes skill..."

"That seems like an excuse to me. It sounds like you're looking down on minstrels whose styles bring in lots of fans."

Is this really a conversation I'm hearing in a fantasy world...?

It was so vivid, it almost felt like it was happening in Japan...

Young band members would've had this kind of conversation for sure...

"Be it skill or proving yourself, you're still worse than the Church of Holy Tears. They actually have technique."

"Th-that's just your opinion, though, Flatorte... See, what's important in music is if you can feel the soul—"

"And there we go. Now you're trying to fool me with your abstract expressions."

Flatorte is relentless!

"P-please stop! I'm doing my best!"

"*Sigh...* Fine. I'll show you what I can do, then. Let me have your lute."

It was the tool of her trade, so Kuku seemed a little nonplussed, but she handed it over.

Please don't suddenly snap it over your knee...

"Are you ready? Watch."

And then Flatorte started strumming a beautiful melody on the lute. Her fingers danced on the strings at such high speed!

What sophisticated technique! And it wasn't just technical; the melody was good, too!

Then Flatorte started singing.

The sunlight on this day of rest just makes me cold instead~ ♪

I'm yawning as I wait for you to come~ ♪

I dropped my glove some time ago~ ♪

So I hope you'll warm my hand in yours~ ♪

Let us fly, fly, fly above the clouds to a quiet place~ ♪

Yeah, yeeeaaah~ ♪

That was a real song! A real and proper song!

And she was good at singing, too! Her voice control was incredible!

Heck, that was quality I'd expect to hear on a TV show!

I almost thought I saw an imaginary drummer and bassist standing behind her.

I knew it—this lute was practically just a guitar. It sounded exactly the same.

The song was over, and the last notes faded.

I inadvertently started clapping. "I didn't know you were so talented, Flatorte! I almost thought I was going to cry!"

"I played a little bit with my friends when I was young. I'm not incredibly skilled, so it's a little embarrassing, though... At most, I'm an above-average amateur."

I knew what she wanted to say. She was good, but that didn't necessarily mean she could make a career out of it.

On the other hand, Kuku's expression was blank.

It was almost as though she had a different song playing in her head. She hadn't come back to reality.

"See, even I, Flatorte, can give such a performance. You say you concentrate on your technique, but you're worse than I am. If you're going to stick with death style, then you should at least raise the standards of your playing. Do you understand better now?"

Kuku was pale. It was almost like she'd frozen to death...

"I-I'm sorry... I will try my hand at many different things, then... I'll stop obsessing over death style..."

"Listen. I know this is my opinion as an outsider, but the reason you don't have any listeners is because your worldview is too peculiar. Why don't you write lyrics that are easier to understand?"

"B-but... I've been performing in this style for so long, I can only write lyrics about blood and poison and destruction and the apocalypse and transient pleasures and devils and knives and drowning fish..."

"You haven't actually written that much about drowning fish, have you?"

"I wrote six songs about them in the past."

Ah, she's the type to use her favorite phrase over and over!

Her other topics were all from the same perspective. It was too narrow. Actually, I was impressed she spent such a long time writing about them. In a way, her desire to stick to the same through line, even if she was running out of things to write about...

Then a good idea came to me.

"I've got it. We'll use the strengths of this environment."

It was a good idea in my head, at least—would it work out?

"We have a big family, so we should make everyone write lyrics!"

Two days later, the whole family brought over the lyrics they each wrote.

But since Flatorte had already performed once, I gave her a pass on this one and asked her to act as a commentator. If I let her get serious, the risk of her being the sole winner was high.

Kuku would improvise a melody to go along with each set of lyrics. She might create a whole new perspective this way.

"All right, we'll start with the first song. These are Laika's lyrics."

"Wah-ha-ha-ha, I, Schifanoia, can sing all words with my gloriously beautiful voice!"

"Okay, it's time to put that character away."

"…Okay. Understood."

And now, the first song.

Kuku started strumming her lute.

"An Ode to Diligence"
Words: Laika
Music: Kuku
The only way to success is by diligently taking one step at a time~ ♪
And once you overcome something, that becomes nothing more than a checkpoint~ ♪

I crossed my arms to make an X. That was my signal to stop.

"Laika, your message is much too direct for lyrics."

"Are they no good…?"

"That's not even a question. Lyrics are poetry. You don't understand poetry. Do it again."

Flatorte, our commentator, relentlessly shot her down.

Laika seemed pretty shocked…

Next was the second song. Halkara seemed very confident in herself. The more confidence Halkara had, the more of a sign it was that things were going to turn south.

"These lyrics are fantastic! This will be very lucrative! Please spread it throughout the town of Nascúte!"

Nascúte was where Halkara's factory was and where Rosalie used to live. Why only there?

"Even if your lyrics are weird, it won't cause any trouble. It's fine. Go ahead; go ahead."

"You're awful, Madam Teacher… However, once you hear these lyrics, I believe you'll understand why I said it'll be lucrative. I do plan on distributing this."

Well then, we'd see what she got. Kuku was the one composing the song, though.

She started strumming her lute again. The intro sounded very poppy.

"Halkara Pharmaceuticals Nutri-Spirits"
Words: Halkara
Music: Kuku

Another round of work today? Nutri-Spirits!~ ♪
You know what to use for a night of cramming! Nutri-Spirits!~ ♪
Nonalcoholic, so it's safe for kids! Nutri-Spirits!~ ♪
A remedy for everything, and it's good for you! Nutri-Spirits!~ ♪
Nutri-Spirits~♪ Nutri-Spirits~♪ Nutri-Spirits~ ♪
Halkara Pharmaceuticals Nutri-Spirits gets you through the day~ ♪

*** * *

I see, so that's where it was going. I get it now.

With a big smile on my face, I made an X with my arms.

"All right, let's go to the next one!"

"Hey! Madam Teacher! At least give me some comments! Ignoring me hurts the most!"

"Then why'd you make an ad jingle?! That's not what we're trying to do here!"

"It's a lucrative song, isn't it?! Nutri-Spirits would rake in the dough with this!"

"It has to be lucrative for the *artist*!"

We're not talking about selling products here!

"Listen, even if by some mistake this ends up a hit, it would just be a one-hit wonder. It'll be old news in two months or so! Seventy-five days is as long as they last!"

"I-if I was a hot topic for two months… I wouldn't mind that…"

Kuku was caving!

You can't! You'll never be even a one-hit wonder if that's your stance from the get-go! You need to have big dreams and big ideals!

"If you were to sing songs that advertise my products while you're on your world tour, I would be ready and willing to hire you as PR rep at Halkara Pharmaceuticals."

"Maybe that's not a bad idea… That might be the right answer to living off my music…"

"Kuku, calm down and think! The first six months might be fine, but three years down the line, I think you'll just repeat the pattern by telling yourself that isn't what you want to do! You'll end up quitting!"

It was a life decision, so I was not going to be shy about interfering.

Being too careful about finding employment was the perfect amount of careful!

I'd died from overwork before, so I would say it out loud!

"Hmph… Madam Teacher, you sure do interfere with me a lot…

My company, business dealings, and treatment of employees are all perfectly legitimate. I even hand out bonuses on time."

"I'm not denying that, and having a more stable livelihood would be a plus for her, but I feel like the change wouldn't be in her music but in her whole line of work..."

I felt like there were plenty of people even in Japan who would sing about destruction then start singing mediocre love songs seven years later. That could be explained by one's musical style gradually getting more universal.

But if she started singing advertising songs for a company, that would be like a cat turning into a dog. It was far from a gradual transition.

"Um, I'd like to decide after seeing the rest of the lyrics," Kuku said hesitantly.

She was right. She couldn't decide when she was only halfway through.

And incidentally, our commentator, Flatorte, didn't seem to have anything to add about it. Guess she didn't have comments this time...

"Next, we'll have the collaboration between Falfa and Shalsha. Aw, you're so cute; this is great."

"Yaaay! Thank you, Mommy!"

"The master of ceremonies is showing favoritism toward a relative! She's treating her daughters differently!" Halkara insisted, but I ignored her.

"We don't need favoritism, because Shalsha is convinced that this song will win. That's because we are participating together. Putting the strength of a hundred thousand with another hundred thousand makes not two hundred thousand but a million."

I didn't quite understand Shalsha's logic, but Kuku was going to play.

"The Field"
Words: Falfa and Shalsha
Music: Kuku
Mister Mantis scares me~ What is he praying for?~ ♪
Mister Grasshopper hops~ His little legs shake as he springs~ ♪
Nature is so big~ And I'm part of nature, too~ ♪

God is big~ Everything lies within the thing most vast~ ♪
What am I?~ I'm not a grasshopper or a mantis, so what am I?~ ♪
I am nothing else, so I must be me, I believe. Even after I have repudiated everything else in the world, that will remain the only thing I can claim. Once I have lost everything, once nothing is left, my self will show itself—the great paradox~ ♪
So in the end, it is what I'll find if I spend an eternity peeling an onion~ ♪
I chase grasshoppers in the field as this runs through my mind~ ♪

Near the end, the lyrics were written without any concern for the melody, so it sounded like a folk song.

Once it finished, the mood had changed.

The first one to speak was Flatorte.

"I thought this would be a more childlike song at first, but…then some theological elements slipped in… Hmm, could this be new territory? It's very avant-garde. It has potential."

"I thought the same…"

It was pretty obvious that Falfa wrote the first half and Shalsha took over from the middle, but as a result, it produced an unusual story-like feel. It seemed to match Kuku's style, too.

And music was originally a mostly religious thing, even used for preaching. It could work.

Kuku seemed dumbfounded for a little bit, but her expression slowly brightened.

"This is wonderful! I don't think there are any minstrels with songs like this in the capital! This trend might be a good thing!"

Falfa jumped and cheered, and Shalsha nodded, somewhat pleased with herself.

To think their lyrics would *actually* win the competition.

"Okay, then. Kuku, why don't you try your minstrel work again, going in that direction?"

"Yes, okay!"

I'd never heard her more energetic.

"With that kind of melody, you could even keep the name Schifanoia. There were probably some mythic motifs to some of your songs about destruction."

"No, since I'll be changing the essence of my musical genre, I'll be changing my moniker, too. I'm thinking 'Encyclopedia, Explorer of All Creation.'"

And the name was still edgy.

"Hmm, that's not really my taste, but I guess your name should stand out... Well, you're the one making the decision anyway."

All right, now we'd decided on the direction of Kuku's future. This was great!

"Wait, please wait! I haven't shown you my lyrics yet!"

Then Rosalie appeared. Oh right, we still had Rosalie!

"Sorry, sorry. It just suddenly started feeling like the grand finale, you know? It's time for Rosalie's lyrics." While Rosalie didn't have a physical body, she could manipulate a pen to write sentences on paper. "I didn't know what would be a good fit, so I wrote about my own experiences."

"Right, that's fine. The point is to broaden the horizons of our minstrel Schifanoia anyway."

"Nothingness"
Words: Rosalie
Music: Kuku
When you stay put for so long, even high noon looks like night ♪
It's so dark, so dark, full of nothing ♪
Am I dead? But even if I'm alive, I'm already dead ♪
I don't know how to smile anymore ♪
I want to die, but I can't—it's just one of those nights ♪

The soft sound of the lute came to an end.

......

It was in the song, too, but that was way too dark. I knew she said it was her own experience, but...

There were lots of songs in Japan with heavy lyrics, but people who committed suicide wouldn't have written songs afterward. It was pretty intense.

"Big Sis, you know I'm having a fun life right now, right? You know I don't actually feel this way, right?" Rosalie added, probably thinking she'd made a mistake.

"Um, Rosalie, I think the listeners would be happier to hear a song with a more positive outlook on life... I'm not taking your past for granted, though..."

...But maybe I had been.

There was nothing wrong with dark songs. It was probably more of a problem to only ever acknowledge happy songs. But this would probably be hard to sing about over and over.

Um, anyway, I want to see how Kuku is reacting to this... I haven't heard her opinion yet.

Tears were streaming down her cheeks. She wasn't outright bawling, but several silent tears dripped from her face.

"What's wrong, Kuku...?"

"I've never... I've never thought of expressions like this... I always—I always sang about...death and destruction, but...they were only words... I mean, I've never died before..."

Yeah, of course not, I thought, but that comment was a little insensitive, so I kept it to myself.

"My words will never be...as strong as those...of someone in pain... even after death... I've been Schifanoia for a long time, but I don't think I ever said anything meaningful..."

Then Kuku finally raised her head.

"I...am going to get rid of the name Schifanoia. In fact, I'm going to get rid of monikers or stage names. I will go by my own name, Kuku!"

In her eyes, I could sense a powerful will to face her troubles. I was sure Kuku would be fine.

"I want to incorporate the trends from Falfa's, Shalsha's, and Rosalie's lyrics and give the listeners something deeper... There's no point in being a minstrel for decades or centuries if I can't do that..."

"Yeah. You're the one who decides where you'll be taking your next step, so I think this is very meaningful."

I didn't know if this path would be easy or not. It might turn out to be thorny and rough. But if it was the path chosen by the one who would walk it, then any obstacle could be endured.

The air in the room suddenly became very emotional. Even Laika and Rosalie were crying.

"All right, I guess that's a wrap for—"

Halkara tapped me on the shoulder.

"We haven't seen your lyrics yet, Madam Teacher. Show them to us, please."

Urgh... I was trying to use my MC position to get out of presenting them...

"You have to. It's only fair."

"Special Love"
Words: Azusa
Music: Kuku
We can go far with our special love~ ♪
Because our destiny~is in! Our! Hands!~ ♪

I had her stop right at the beginning.

I let Flatorte do the commenting, since they were lyrics I'd written myself. Well, more like Flatorte took over commenting entirely.

"Conventional. The theme is clichéd; I get a strong impression that these were thrown together, like a patchwork quilt of lyrics the writer had heard from other places. The emotions of the speaker aren't represented at all. Is the singer of these words actually glad to be in love?"

"Okay, enough! I know they're embarrassing, too!"

I wrote a song about romance because I wanted something easy to understand, but in reality, it felt way off. I'd tried to just sweep it under the rug, but Flatorte wouldn't let me.

And so, Kuku made the splendid decision to live on as a minstrel and choose what kind of minstrel she would be.

◇

Kuku stayed in the house in the highlands for a while, writing songs.

According to her, she couldn't write at all when she was in a slump, but here the songs just came to her one after the other. Even she was surprised.

She told me about it as we sat at the table having a snack.

"Oh yeah, I think that makes sense. There's no entertainment here at all. It's night and day compared to the royal capital, at least."

There weren't any houses around us, after all, and even if we went all the way to the village, they sold only daily necessities. That meant there were few temptations, and the only thing to do was what you were supposed to do.

"I guess that's true, but... Oh, I didn't mean to insult this land!"

"You don't have to apologize for that."

Kuku was a particularly timid person, although that wasn't strange; there were a number of similarly introverted people involved in music.

Introverts paid more mind to things that normal people wouldn't notice. To put a positive spin on it, they were more in tune with emotions.

Maybe that was why she had so much trouble going in an aggressive direction with Schifanoia...

"If I'm stuck, I just walk around the highlands. And then whatever's sticking just goes away. That's happened many times now. I've been writing every day."

"Oh yeah. It's just a plain old highland here, but when you walk around, your mood starts getting much better, doesn't it?"

No one would feel dispirited living an easy life in this hilltop house anyway, but when the occasional bad mood struck, I would take a walk outside.

And strangely, I would always feel motivated again.

"How many songs have you written?"

"Seventeen. A few I'm not very satisfied with, though."

Sitting with us, Flatorte commented, "You could do a whole show on your own with that." Minstrel performances were long.

"Um, truly, I thank all of you...for everything you've done for me...," Kuku said, clasping her hands before her face. Her gentle personality was just oozing from her. It was hard to imagine she'd been screaming about destruction.

But my heart clenched to hear it.

"I'd only be bothering you if I stayed here, so I should head back to the capital soon..."

Well, that was the next step. That was the promise we'd made at the beginning.

Kuku was a minstrel, so she couldn't live in the countryside forever.

There weren't enough people to make an audience for her here.

"Sure. But if you come back on tour, drop by the house in the highlands, okay? Actually, you should visit your home here on purpose."

With tears brimming in her widened eyes, Kuku said, "Yes, I will!"

"You'll put on a good show. As long as you do that, it'll work out," Flatorte said, the air of a teacher about her.

"Yes, thank you for all your help, Miss Flatorte!"

"Of course. And to be honest, you have no musical talent."

I almost fell backward out of my chair.

Kuku looked like she was going to cry for a different reason now.

"But success in the world isn't determined by your talent." Flatorte wasn't joking around at all as she continued. "So there might be a chance that you are successful. First, you fight! Even if your weapon is different, you will keep on fighting!"

"Yes! I will keep on fighting as a minstrel!"

Oh, there was a real friendship blooming here.

"Tell me when you're going to the capital. I, Flatorte, will take you back as a dragon."

I could tell there was a hint of sadness in her expression. Partings were hard for everyone.

"Thank you. I'll be sure to—"

Knock knock, knock knock.

Someone was at the door.

I had a pretty good guess as to who it was from the bold knocking as I went to the door and opened it.

There was Beelzebub. She had a lot of stuff with her today.

"I've obtained some good alcohol, so I've brought it. Let us drink together!"

"You're here all the time, aren't you? What about your work?"

"I have taken care to give it all to my under— I mean, I have finished it all."

"I really want to tell you to stop pushing all your work onto your subordinates, but you're the agricultural minister. I guess it's better for the agricultural minister to delegate instead of doing it all on her own."

"I am doing my part, too, you know. I rest on the weekends and holidays. I spend them with Falfa and Shalsha."

That was her goal? Well, I could understand, though.

I couldn't just chase her off, so Beelzebub entered.

Of course, since Kuku was in the house, I did simple introductions.

"Oh, a minstrel, are you? Then we shall have you play some songs at our drinking party," Beelzebub said as though it was a given. High-and-mighty might be her style, but she was overdoing it.

"Hey! Can you stop acting so unreasonable? Everyone who lives in this house is family. I don't want you treating her like some street musician you saw in town, okay?"

"But minstrels are for adding life to banquets, are they not? What is so wrong with requesting work for such an honest reason? I will pay, of course."

There were people who did that sort of thing in royal courts, sure…

"Miss Azusa, I'll do it. If you'll let me, please." Kuku's expression was full of confidence. "I want someone who's never heard my music before to listen to me. To see if I can keep going as my new self."

If she was saying it, then I had no reason to stop her. "Okay, Beelzebub. Kuku is going to bring you to tears now!"

"What? I asked for this during the drinking party, not now. First, I must give your daughters gifts."

Like a slap in the face...

It was less of a drinking party and more of a dinner plus Beelzebub. There was alcohol, so she probably wouldn't complain.

The stuff she'd brought was pretty strong. I only had a sip, and that was still too much.

"Isn't there too much alcohol in this...? It burns, like fire..."

"I don't quite understand the concept of alcohol content, but I understand when you call it fire. This was made by lizardman artisans on Flame Mountain, where fire constantly spews from the ground. It's called the Great Salamander."

"Yeah, this is spicy... I hope Halkara doesn't get sick from this, too."

Halkara waved both her hands in denial. "I cannot drink this, Madam Teacher!"

"You heard her. Don't you have anything lighter?"

"Most of what I have is hot and spicy. I have one that's essentially water. It's called Essentially Water."

I wasn't sure if this was peculiar to demons or Beelzebub's own character, but these drinks were only the extremes.

Laika had a little bit of the weaker alcohol, too. That probably meant it was all right. Age-wise, everyone in the family was an adult. Laika drank, too.

"I, Flatorte, am fine with the spicy drink."

In our house, Flatorte was the best when it came to holding her liquor. She glugged it down with such vigor, it might as well have been water. It seemed like it was fairly high-grade, so it felt a bit like a waste.

"Mommy, can Falfa drink, too?"

The two sisters reacted differently to alcohol—Shalsha didn't even look at it, while Falfa seemed interested.

"Absolutely not, Falfa. You can't have any until you're grown up."

Even though they were fifty years in age, their bodies were too small, so I didn't allow them to drink. Conversely, Laika and Flatorte were enormous dragons, so they wouldn't have any problems even if they looked ten years old.

"Awww, Falfa wants to grow up!"

Beelzebub didn't seem happy with that statement. "Falfa, you do not need to grow up at all. Stay as you are. Being an adult is terribly boring. It is more fun being a child," she said with a grave expression.

I had a feeling this sort of education could prove problematic...

"Awww, but Falfa isn't like a big sister at all. I'm not much bigger than Shalsha..." Falfa deflated as she explained herself.

That made sense. She had her own earnest reasons.

"I don't know how to be a big sister... I'm not much faster, and Shalsha is smart about other things, so I thought maybe I could lead when it came to alcohol..."

Beelzebub was getting worked up. "Oooh! She's too cute! I must adopt her as my own!" But I ignored her. No way would I give her up for adoption.

"Don't worry. You do act like a big sister every now and then, Falfa."

It was times like these that I had to give her a good consoling.

"Yeah..."

"And if you do drink, you'll end up like that."

At the far end of the room, Halkara had collapsed, her stomach sloppily exposed.

"I thought it was mostly water, so I drank too much too quickly. It's like I'm drunk enough for ten thousand large armies and it's hitting all at once... I feel like I'm going to throw up, but nothing's happening... It's the worst... Uuugh..."

Rosalie placed a damp towel on her forehead, but it slipped from its spot. Halkara looked like she was on her deathbed.

"Okay, maybe Falfa won't drink..."

Good examples of what *not* to do did have some power over children... Halkara was a great example for that. But our great example needed to learn a bit more herself. Some people just wore themselves down whenever they drank, didn't they?

"Erm, I hate to interrupt while you chat, but...I think it's about time that we have Kuku perform for us...," Flatorte said, and then I remembered!

Oh, shoot! I completely forgot!

Kuku had a hesitant look on her face that said, *Should I say something? Maybe I should keep waiting... I wanted to speak up when the conversation lulled, but it just keeps going...*

Ahhh, Kuku is so shy! She can't come out and say she's starting!

"Sorry, sorry. I'll listen to your song. Depending on how I evaluate you, I may even invite you to the demons' music festival."

"What's this music festival?"

I'd never heard of this event. I could imagine the gist of what it was, though.

"You guys have a pretty high standard of civilization, don't you? You have performances and stuff."

"It is not a performance. We have no miserable events such as that. It is a music festival, one large event that takes place throughout the whole of Vanzeld town." Beelzebub took offense to my expression.

"Oh, is it one of those things where there are lots of performances at once? Like ensembles come out and march on the field?"

"Hmph, there are some of those, yes, but I feel you do not have a grasp of the fundamental concept. The music festival is to confirm that the demon king controls sound on behalf of the demons."

After that explanation, the atmosphere suddenly changed.

"Do you understand? Sound is everywhere in this world. Voices hawking wares as you walk around town, animals rustling through the brush in the forest, and even when you meditate in a quiet room, you can hear a soft ringing in your ears that signals an absence of sound. Nowhere will you find true silence."

The idea that the ringing itself was a sound was a point of view unique to the demons.

"In short, sound is just as important an element as the four great elements. The music festival is to confirm whether the demon king, as the ruler of the demons, is properly managing sound."

I see… They regarded sound with great importance. It was like universities in Europe during the Middle Ages treating music not like an art but as a basic science…

"So it is not just one or two performances like you mentioned. It is a celebration with a more fundamental meaning. Get it now?"

"Yes, I get it now. There's a strong religious implication to it."

"It is customary that the demon king performs music at the main event. Oh, you all might be invited this time."

Pecora would definitely invite us. Even if it was for the purpose of some joke of hers.

"Erm, I'd like Kuku to perform sometime soon…"

"You're right! Kuku, Flatorte, I'm sorry!"

Kuku held her lute and stood by the table.

This was the stage for Kuku, reborn.

"And now I will play you a few songs."

She started strumming her lute.

Compared to that intense genre Kuku had been playing at first—death style, was it?—this was completely different.

A thoughtful mood filled the room.

We were probably supposed to eat as we listened, but everyone was focused on her.

We were listening so intently, no one clapped or said anything between songs.

Flatorte had said something that could be generously interpreted as, *Talent alone doesn't make a minstrel*, but I understood what that meant.

All the songs Kuku was playing now had words that she had

carefully chosen and woven together on her own. They stirred us easily; they went straight to the heart.

What she had been doing before might have been restricted by the genre she was playing in, which meant she had to be very successful within the genre for it to be worth anything.

But since she was a poet before she was a singer, she had to be able to do as poets did and speak in her own words.

There were sometimes too many words in her poems, so they didn't exactly fit the melody, but they reminded me a little of folk songs I'd heard in Japan before. They had their own unique merits.

After she played five songs in a row, her performance was finished.

At the end, Kuku bowed slowly. "Thank you for listening."

She might've made a few mistakes here and there, but she looked accomplished.

Like the whole family had been suddenly brought back to reality, we all burst into applause.

And what did Beelzebub think? I hoped she liked it. Beelzebub suddenly stood from her chair.

"That was wonderful!!! Excellent!!!"

Woo! It really must have struck her heart!

"To be honest, I thought this would not be as impressive, only good enough for side entertainment. I did not expect it would be so lovely..."

Those rude remarks were a little too honest.

"Mm, it was good. Very good. First, I shall give you fifty thousand koinne." Beelzebub whipped out coins of the demon koinne currency.

"Ah, if possible, my preferred unit is gold. I would have to exchange this."

The value was practically the same as gold, so it might as well have been in gold.

"Very well. Here, fifty thousand gold."

And she paid it. Getting paid for your work sure is great.

"Thank you... If I could make fifty thousand gold per day working ten days a month, I believe I could live a stable life..."

Kuku also seemed touched to have actually gotten paid. Her days as Schifanoia must have been really tough. I never really felt like giving her money after hearing any of her old songs...

"And please do come to the music festival. If you are successful, you may just find your fortune," Beelzebub said. It sounded suspicious, but demons were an excitable bunch. Maybe Kuku really would get a sudden windfall. Beelzebub retrieved documents on the music festival from her things and handed them to Kuku.

"Um, how might I be able to get to the demon castle...?"

"If you'll participate, then we'll have someone come get you."

A leviathan or some other method of fast travel would come for her.

"If you're all right with me... I'm a nobody, though..." At that moment, Kuku became unsure.

"Whether you are a nobody or a somebody in the human world does not matter. A majority of the demons know nothing about anyone's reputation in the human world anyway."

"I understand. Then if you're all right with me going, I'll go..."

Kuku had performed in front of people before. She would keep going forward.

"Mm. I do not know which stage we'll use yet, but you'll likely be performing before anywhere between ten to twenty thousand people."

"Wha—?! That many?!"

That was way too dramatic of a change. If you multiplied her original audiences by a hundred, it still wouldn't come close...

"Ah, do you think...you could put me in a smaller venue, maybe for about three hundred...?"

Oh no! Kuku's cracking under the pressure! She's sounding weak again!

"Every venue in the music festival is full of people. There will be no place with only three hundred. You will do this. All you have to do is play about twenty of those songs you just did, no?" Beelzebub patted Kuku on the shoulder. "Believe in yourself. Your feelings have reached the heart of your listener. I know well how serious you are. There won't be any problems!"

"O-okay!" Kuku answered, overpowered by Beelzebub's energy.

"All right, all riiight! You will do your best. And now I shall take a bath."

Beelzebub was the kind of person to enthusiastically use her status as the guest to take the first bath.

I wondered if she would announce that she was moving in soon...

"You will come with me, Falfa and Shalsha."

"Okaaay!" "Sure."

And so Beelzebub left the room.

To put it frankly, I wasn't going to disturb them, since her goal was to play with my daughters.

On the other hand, Kuku started shaking after Beelzebub left.

"An audience of ten to twenty thousand... I couldn't...I couldn't perform in front of that many even if I faced the wall... There are too many zeros in that number for me to understand..."

"I know how you feel, but this is your chance. Make it count!"

All I could do was support her.

"Um... I'll practice really hard, so would it be all right to stay here a little longer...? I'd have to work if I go back to the capital, and I won't be able to squeeze in any practice..."

That was a very clear reason. The girl sounded like she really didn't have any money.

"Got it. We'll feed you as much as you need, so practice hard, okay?"

Kuku gripped her lute. "Okay!" she said.

It seemed our life with Kuku wasn't over just yet.

FALFA AND SHALSHA

Spirit sisters born from a conglomeration of slime souls. Falfa, the older sister, is a carefree girl who's honest about her own feelings. Shalsha, the younger sister, is considerate and attentive to others. They both love their mother, Azusa.

HALKARA

A young elf woman and Azusa's second apprentice. Everyone in the family (particularly Azusa) admires her periodic bouts of maturity and her enviably perfect looks… That doesn't change her role as the family member with a knack for screwing up.

BEELZEBUB

A high-ranking demon known as the Lord of the Flies. She frequently shuttles between the demon realm and the house in the highlands, both to get the Nutri-Spirits Halkara makes and to dote on Falfa and Shalsha as if they were her nieces. She's Azusa's reliable "big sister" surrogate.

A few days later, someone of an unfamiliar dragon race came to my house.

I asked Laika afterward, and she said it was a wyvern. Like the one making deliveries to the apothecary at the World Tree, right? I still wasn't sure about all the small differences among wyverns and drakes and other dragons.

Of course, the wyvern wouldn't have come out here for no good reason.

It brought an invitation from the demon king.

That's it?! All for this?!

The date was written on the second page. Fatla and Vania would apparently take us there. I guess I'd be treated as a national guest as long as I was acting as the demon king's older sister.

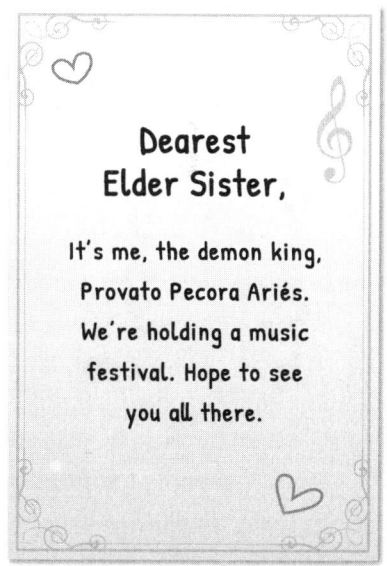

Dearest Elder Sister,

It's me, the demon king, Provato Pecora Ariés. We're holding a music festival. Hope to see you all there.

Incidentally, Kuku had been writing songs and practicing harder than ever before since Beelzebub came to visit. Almost to the point where I couldn't just waltz into her room. What was once a spare space in the house had completely transformed into a studio.

"Kuku's been improving a lot. I knew it—she would never gain the skill if she did not practice her hardest. She must be determined to give it her all now," Flatorte said, listening to the sounds of Kuku's practice coming from her room.

It was teatime for Flatorte, Laika, and me. My daughters weren't interested in tea by itself, so they didn't come. Halkara was at work. I didn't see Rosalie nearby, but she was somewhere around.

"I'm an amateur, but I can tell she's been improving."

Laika loved people who were always striving for self-improvement, because she had the same personality type.

"Kuku has the patience to do the same thing over and over. Had that patience been directed in just a slightly different direction, she could have made so much more progress," Flatorte remarked about her music. "Some hard work doesn't produce good results, and some does. Kuku had trouble telling which was which, but she's been improving rapidly now that we've corrected her."

What she said could be applied to many things, not just music.

There were people who made efforts that weren't effective or didn't have much point.

In middle school, I had a classmate who poured her heart into making her notes look immaculate, but her grades were average.

The point of notes was to make sure you didn't forget anything you heard in class. They didn't need to be nice and neat, like merchandise. Though they definitely should be clear instead of muddled, you should be able to understand them, as the one who wrote them.

This classmate of mine ended up making it her goal to take perfect notes. If she'd just shifted her enthusiasm over to raising her grades, I was sure she would've done better.

"In that case, that means you have no patience and no stamina to work hard over long periods of time." Laika stabbed a thorn straight into Flatorte.

"Wh-wh-wh-wh-wh-what! What does that mean?!"

"I mean, in recent memory, you would go and fight my elder sister Leila, wouldn't you? Perhaps you should've spent a little more time preparing to defeat her?"

"Well, that's what you do... I'm impressed by those who live their lives thinking of who they will defeat that day! That's why I thought it was perfect to go bully her whenever it occurred to me!"

This was getting strange. I didn't know if I was convinced or not...

People who are always yelling, "Down with so-and-so!" sure are a problem, but please don't just go bully people when you feel like it.

That being said, I felt a little love now in the relationship between the red and blue dragons, like rival neighborhoods in a sports competition.

Of course, it was still a fight between dragons, so it was on a much more unusual scale. Plus, some of the younger ones really would take it too far. The rivalry was a big problem.

"Hmph, don't push me too much today. Fine. Whoever is luckier in their horoscope is the winner!"

"Very well. I accept."

This showdown was a little *too* peaceful.

Maybe they get along so well because they're both dragons...

We could still hear Kuku's lute from her room. And unlike during her Schifanoia era, there were lots of quiet songs to ensure a reasonable noise level.

The snippets of music must have grabbed Flatorte's attention again.

"I had a feeling. Kuku went all the way to the capital, so she probably wants to erect a bronze statue in her hometown."

I felt like I'd heard a similar expression before in the past. It probably meant coming home with great honor and glory.

"Those who go to the capital for art sometimes do, don't they? Perhaps it's hard to say one accomplished anything there without becoming famous."

"I've seen plenty of minstrels like that... I wonder what Leapfrog and White Lightning and Arsakes are all up to now..."

I didn't know any of these minstrel names.

"They say only one in fifty gets a bronze statue. Oh—home..."

Flatorte suddenly seemed to remember something.

Now that she mentioned it, she hadn't gone home once since coming to live in the house in the highlands...

"R-right! I didn't have the time to go home, so I forgot!"

"Then good thing you remembered, right? You can go home—or wait, can you?"

I seemed to remember a rule that she wasn't allowed to leave my side while she was living here.

"No... And I want to go home, but at the same time I don't. It's a very complicated feeling..."

"What do you mean?"

"I would be a failed dragon returning home... All those people looking at me..."

Flatorte's gaze was directed straight down. *So that's why...*

Only she could understand how that would feel, I suppose.

Since I had been an office employee, I could go to my parents' house to soothe my everyday weariness, but I had a steady job. Not that it did any good in the long run; steady job or not, the overwork led to my death...

"Okay, so if you did go home, would people look at you coldly, then?"

I would be the one responsible for that, so I asked hesitantly.

"At the very least, I wasn't treated any differently after we attacked the red dragon village and lost. The blue dragons as a whole were the losers anyhow. We are equal on that front."

"So they didn't push all the blame on you, then. Your society is very accepting, Flatorte. More accepting than the company I worked for, at least."

They'd always had a scapegoat ready for these things.

"Lady Azusa, as far as I know, power is the law among blue dragons.

I believe that since the whole clan was recognized as weak, they had no choice but to grin and bear it, despite their regrets," Laika offered.

Flatorte nodded weakly, so Laika was probably right. Flatorte looked up to me with puppy eyes and kept going. "But right now, I, Flatorte, must absolutely obey my mistress's orders... There are a number of blue dragons who would find that disgraceful..."

"Oh! I didn't know. I feel bad..."

Since I'd petted Flatorte's horns, she had no choice but to live with me.

And this injustice began with the mischief-loving demon king, Pecora.

But...I was glad that Flatorte had become a member of the family, and I had a lot of feelings about it, too. I even wanted to thank Pecora sometimes.

"So which is it? Do you want to go home or do you not?" Laika asked her straight.

"Hey, this isn't a simple question. I've thought and thought about it. I've thought all about it, but I still don't know..."

"But you must decide if you're going home; otherwise, you will never get there regardless. If you just wait for a chance, it will never work out perfectly. Even you said that Kuku couldn't have just waited for her big break without making some changes."

Laika's argument went straight for the heart.

But her sincerity worked with Flatorte. I was sure she saw that Laika was seriously thinking about her as a dragon.

"I—I guess I want to go home... I at least want to tell my parents that I'm living happily with my mistress."

And this was the conclusion Flatorte found after some deliberation.

"Great! Then I'll go with you. You won't be able to go otherwise, right?"

"Yes, you're right, but... There are plenty of blue dragons who don't know of your strength firsthand, so could you exude an aura of immense power, please?"

I didn't quite understand what Flatorte was saying.

"If every blue dragon knows that no one is a match for you, Mistress, then people might think that I, Flatorte, have no choice but to continue living in the house in the highlands. That might relieve some pressure on me, I think."

This wasn't something she could say loud and proud, so she was talking in a hushed voice, but I understood her intention.

If they recognized me as a power no blue dragon could defeat, then no one would think that Flatorte was serving me because she was weak.

"But won't I be playing the role of a villain, then…?"

"That's all right. We blue dragons value power as our standard of justice. We even believe that as long as we work hard, we might be able to win our disputes with the red dragons."

I wondered why they had such a monarchical mentality, but did dragons even have monarchs in the first place?

"Understood. Then let's pick a good time to go."

"Let's go right now."

"Wait, seriously? I know they say good deeds should be done quickly, but—"

"Lady Azusa, I will go with you." Laika told us she was coming along.

"I don't mind, but wouldn't you be traveling into enemy territory?"

"That may be true, but… I thought it unfair that she gets to travel with you, Lady Azusa…," she muttered.

Oooh! She's so cute! Just like I knew my little sister would be!

"You can come if you want. I'm not carrying you." Flatorte was obviously unhappy with this.

"That's fine. I can fly."

I rode on Flatorte, and we headed for the blue dragon village.

If we left immediately, we would apparently get there around dinnertime.

At times like these, perhaps it's best to leave the moment we decide to do something. For example, one could usually get to anywhere within Japan in the same day if you took the bullet train or a plane. You could even visit home.

But people didn't. Not only did it cost money, but it was hard to decide when, which inevitably led to putting it off.

We could go home whenever we wanted, so we ended up doing so only once or twice a year.

We soon landed just at the entrance of the blue dragon village.

My first thought after landing was:

"It's cold! I mean, it's covered in snow!"

"Yes. The snow never melts here."

Flatorte, now back in her human form, seemed totally content.

On the other hand, Laika had her arms wrapped around herself like me, trying to withstand the cold.

"Then let's go to the village. Everyone is typically in their human form, so it shouldn't seem too strange."

We walked for a little bit, and we came across a small smattering of houses sitting at a much higher elevation than my own house.

There was a sign at the entrance that just said, THIS IS THE BLUE DRAGON VILLAGE.

As we walked along what was probably the main street, we came to a large square at the center.

There were several roads extending in a radial pattern from the square.

Even farther in, there was a building atop a staircase of about a hundred steps. It was probably a religious institution or some kind of fort. If this were Japan, that's where a shrine or temple would be.

"It's more humanlike than the red dragon village was. It's not much different from a human village."

"Indeed. We live our lives in human form in consideration of efficiency. There is not much to be gained by showing off our dragon forms. That's what makes us different from the pretentious red dragons."

"Why must you insult us for that?" Laika objected. Understandable.

"Flatorte, don't explicitly go looking for fights like that. Now apologize."

"Urgh... Mistress, it was a joke..."

"A rude joke. And if someone told you that blue dragons are idiots without any foresight, you'd be angry, too, right?"

"Ugh... S-sorry..." Flatorte gave in quickly and apologized to Laika.

This is one of those problems you should solve as soon as you notice it.

"It's so empty in here."

There was no one around as far as I could tell at a glance. No one on the main street, at least.

"Could they be holed up inside because it's cold...?" Laika asked, but she was speaking from the perspective of a red dragon with little tolerance for the chill.

"But there's no lights on anywhere at all, even though it's getting dark outside."

That's right—we arrived at night, not during the day, and yet nothing was lit.

"Oh, I think we were too late. Everyone's asleep already."

"Wait, asleep?"

"Yes. Once it gets dark, blue dragons quickly eat dinner and go straight to sleep. For example—"

Flatorte turned the corner onto a side street, chose a random house, and peeked inside.

That's not very considerate; is she breaking the law...? She was like a thief casing the premises.

"Look. Everyone's asleep."

We peered through the gloom and, sure enough, everyone was in bed.

"It's not that late, though... It's only just past six..." Laika was bewildered. She wasn't exactly a night owl herself, but it was still way too early...

As we stood there, my stomach growled.

"Hey, is there at least a bar or something that's open late here?"

"No."

That was fast!

Oh no. It feels like we've been stranded in the middle of nowhere...

"There's nothing to do here, and it'll be pitch-black soon. Why don't we go home and sleep now?"

"But your family's already asleep, aren't they...? We'd be sleeping there before we even say hello... I dunno..."

"If I sleep there, they won't think the red dragons are trying to start something, will they...?"

Laika was worried about that, too.

It'd be one complicated homecoming if we came back while her family was asleep and invited ourselves to spend the night!

"I was thinking that maybe we should stay at an inn here in town, even if it costs money... Sleeping in an unfamiliar house stresses me out...," Laika suggested. I was tempted to agree...

I didn't want her parents to get the wrong idea about us, so I was reluctant to sleep there.

"No inns, either." Flatorte's response came easily.

"There's nothing here!"

"Well, there are no highways in town. We don't get travelers. We don't need inns."

This place is worse than I thought... Even Flatta has more than this!

"So then what industry was it based around?"

"There's no industry here. Whenever we need money, we go to a human settlement, do some physical labor to earn it, then come back. Otherwise, we go to undeveloped mountains and hunt boars and whatnot whenever we feel like it."

"Um, I think you should stop this aimless lifestyle and live with a little more culture."

What Laika said sounded dangerously similar to an insult, but it was the truth...

"We do have culture. See, we have a shrine at the top of the staircase, and we hold festivals there several times a year. These festivals are rather intense. Some people get so worked up that a brawl usually breaks out. People are inevitably injured, but that just adds to the excitement!"

Laika stared at Flatorte coolly.

I remembered when the blue dragons attacked the red dragons.

They'd suddenly come to attack back then, too, and it reminded me of something. These blue dragons lived like delinquent high schoolers!

Hey, I heard the red dragons are holding a wedding. → That pisses me off; let's attack 'em!

I'm hungry. → Let's hunt some boar.

Man, I got no money. → I'm off to get some dough.

I lost to someone who's real good in a fight. → Whoa, insane! So much respect! We'll follow you forever!

We should have a festival. → WOOOO, LET'S GO!

But delinquent kids wouldn't go to sleep so early. That was the only difference.

Still, their lifestyle didn't seem particularly stable. There was no concept of planning here.

This typically wasn't sustainable, but dragons were powerful enough to pull it off.

"Lady Azusa, I realize that what I'm about to say is rather selfish, but I will head for the nearest town and stay at an inn there."

Laika's expression was tense. She was serious.

"I guess I should do the same... I don't really want to sleep in someone's house before saying hello... We'll come back again tomorrow..."

"What?! Seriously?!"

In the end, along with Flatorte, we flew thirty minutes to a town at the foot of the mountains to stay there for the night.

That night, while Flatorte was in the bath, Laika complained to me.

"Lady Azusa, it is not a mistake that the blue and red dragons do not get along. It is entirely the fault of those idiots. We had no major connections in the past; they would just come to fight us because they thought we were acting snooty."

It reminded me of punks in high school going to rile up the kids at the school next door...

"I can't say this too loudly, but I think it's possible that the reason she can't get married is because the other dragons avoid her... Blue dragons are the absolute problem children of all dragons..."

Why did I have to be so involved in interpersonal relationships even in a different world?

Then Flatorte came out of the bath, steam rising from her skin.

"Phew! The water's great. That was a wonderful bath."

Laika and I kept our mouths shut.

I couldn't shake the feeling that we'd run into trouble again tomorrow...

The next morning, nine AM—we went back to visit the blue dragon village.

But there was still no one walking around.

"Oh, blue dragons are usually only active between ten and five, so that might be why."

What are they, a shop in the sticks...?

But they were probably awake, at least, so we went to Flatorte's house.

There were two people there with horns, likely her parents. They didn't seem like ruffians. And since dragons aged slowly, they looked like humans in their thirties.

"Oh, Flatorte, you're home!"

"I heard a rumor that someone touched your horns!"

Flatorte's father and mother greeted her, and their faces told me immediately that they were overjoyed.

But Flatorte didn't know how to react upon seeing her parents. "I-I'm home…" She faltered.

This was no different from a human homecoming.

"You lost to a red dragon last time. Well, these things happen. You can't fight anymore according to the rules, but that's fine. There's nothing wrong with going for a challenge, you know. It's normal to beat 'em up when you get angry."

Her father sounded both reasonable and totally unreasonable at once.

Don't tell your daughter to beat people up when she's angry!

"That's right. You did it because you thought it was a good idea, so there's nothing to feel sorry about. Don't worry about shame or anything like that. The chickens who wouldn't go to fight are the ones who should be ashamed."

Her mother was being encouraging, but something was weird here! I wished they wouldn't recommend violence.

"This is my current mistress, Lady Azusa, the super-powerful Witch of the Highlands. And this is the strongest of the red dragons, Laika."

It was weird hearing about our strength as part of an introduction.

And we were all of a sudden being introduced to not just any blue dragons but to Flatorte's parents.

How would they react…? I wondered if they saw me as the nasty woman enslaving their precious daughter…

The color in her parents' eyes changed.

"You're the Witch of the Highlands?! Wow! You're real! You're the real thing! Let's fight later!"

"You're much slenderer than I thought you'd be, Miss Witch of the Highlands! Please autograph the wall! Let us fight later!"

"Uh, I hope you don't mind me asking, but why do you want to fight?!"
That's not what you want to say to someone you just met!

"And you must be, like, the red dragon boss, huh? Sorry about before. Let's fight next time."

"We can't have an all-out brawl, but I suppose we could have a sort of scrimmage in a safer environment. Why don't we fight?"

Laika's face was twitching as she held it in a strained position. "A-all right...," she said as she bowed.

It was like a young girl from a posh household had come to play at her uncouth friend's house...

"Now that we're here again, I'm going to show you two around the village. We don't have any shops, though."

"Thanks..."

Afterward, blue dragons in human form started coming out into the village, and everyone who saw Flatorte came to say hello.

I was glad they didn't appear to be making fun of her for serving me. But—

"You're the Witch of the Highlands! Let's fight later." "I'm a nobody, really, but we should fight!" "Missy, missy, fight me!"

As of now, one hundred blue dragons had asked me to fight!

"Lady Azusa, I understand it's racist to claim that elves are obnoxious when they drink, since I can assume there are elves who don't drink as well."

I had a feeling she was thinking of Halkara with that example, but I would ignore that part.

"However, in this situation, saying that blue dragons always ask for a fight is simply a fact. Would that make it all right to say so?"

"I don't see why not. I can't think of anyone around who would be insulted by that."

Flatorte didn't even seem to think anything was strange about it. "I was uneasy on the way back here, but I'm glad nothing's changed."

Were the blue dragons an aggressive people?

It really wasn't an exaggeration to say they believed violence could solve anything...

As we wandered around the village, the number of people around us grew.

I could tell all eyes were on us, since outsiders rarely ever came.

"Mistress, everyone seems to want to test your strength, so would you fight with some of them here?" Flatorte asked me. We could make *fight* the word of the year.

"First, let me be honest: I don't want to. There's nothing to gain from it."

Someone who would want to test their strength couldn't lead a slow life in the highlands for three hundred years.

"But everyone's expecting me to... Some of them look really excited, too... I can't refuse, so I'll do it."

Someone must've heard, because there was a yell: "The Witch of the Highlands who Flatorte serves said she'd fight!"

There came a cheer.

At that moment, I was experiencing the hardships of cultural exchange.

I mean, it was weird for an entire small village to challenge me to a good-natured fight.

And so we set the stage for the fight in the square.

It would've been fine and easy if this was arm wrestling or something, but before I knew it, a whole row of enormous bluish dragons was waiting. Guess this was going to be a serious battle.

It seemed like the entire village was out spectating, some in human form and some in dragon form. There were even some who were still dressed in their pajamas and others waving flags around.

A temporary tent was set up by the square, which became our waiting room.

"Mistress, the standard is to go all out, if that's all right. There is not a single blue dragon who would hold a grudge against you if they lost.

But please just don't touch their horns. The village would fall apart if everyone was to become your servant."

"Yep, I'll keep that in mind..."

If I ended up as the Witch of the Highlands with thirty blue dragon underlings, my peaceful life would be ruined forever...

Laika watched the energetic goings-on with a sour look.

"Lady Azusa, please beat them senseless. She may grow to scorn you if you don't."

Laika was looking straight at Flatorte.

That was possible. If I wasn't a big deal, then that would mean that Flatorte was no big deal. I had to keep her family from being insulted.

"And if someone thinks they have a sliver of a chance at winning, still more might come to fight you. There are non-fighting pacts agreed on between dragons, but none have anything like that with you, Lady Azusa. They might come to our house in the highlands every day, to fight you for the sake of killing time..."

Yes, it was cold outside, but a shiver still ran down my spine.

"Fight with everything you have."

I'll show them that they're no match for me. That was my only choice.

"It seems it's almost time now. I, Flatorte, will act as judge."

"I think that might not be entirely fair, but I just need to have a sweeping victory, then."

I went to the square. The cheers were so loud, but that was because there were so many in dragon form. Some dragons were watching the fight from the sky, so they cast large shadows everywhere.

"The first match is with Flatorte's mother—Cainresq, Cainresq!"

The dragon standing at the front stepped forward.

"I can't just fight one of your parents right from the get-go!"

"Well, I'd like to fight you fresh before you get tired, so I asked my daughter to put me first."

I didn't know what to make of her exercising her influence over the judge to make requests. And she called me *fresh*, like some fish, so that bothered me.

"Let the match begin!"

I ran straight toward the dragon, and she was running right at me. It was perfect.

Don't breathe ice on me.

"Ready and *go!*"

Before she could, I slammed my fist into her, right about where her stomach was.

Wham! A nice resilient impact struck my arm.

The dragon flew high up above the clouds—actually, it wasn't *that* far, but she made a nice parabola as she flew through the sky then landed somewhere outside the village.

"Ma, can you get up? Nah. All right, victory goes to my mistress!"

Flatorte raised my hand high over my head. I guess I just needed to keep this up.

There came a great cheer (more like a roar, since they were dragons) from the crowd. As long as they were enjoying it.

"All right, the next opponent will be Flatorte's father—Armeshtan, Armeshtan!"

First her mom, and now her dad?! Can't you be a little fairer?!

But maybe this is fair, since she's making her connections so obvious...?

"It's been ages since I could cut loose! Get ready, great Witch!"

They sure were a hot-blooded bunch... I thought of all the troubles Laika and the red dragons had gone through.

This time, her father went for a Cold Breath attack right from the start, so I blocked it with Flame magic.

"Wha—! Such power! She didn't even cast anything or use a magic circle!" Someone in the audience shouted like a commentator.

"Sure. The most general way of blocking Cold Breath is to use Flame magic. But drawing a magic circle or casting a spell wouldn't be fast enough, so it's not an effective means of stopping an instant attack like Cold Breath. Meaning this witch is a real powerhouse!"

Don't know who that was, but thanks for the play-by-play.

Right, so nothing would happen if I stayed on the defensive the whole time. I immediately closed the gap between us, and with that acceleration, I kicked!

He didn't go flying this time. He just leaned and then toppled right over.

"Urgh... What might... My daughter could never win against this... That was an overwhelming attack..."

I'm so glad you understand.

I could hear people cheering again: "Amazing!" I could somehow see how power decided what was just. As I defeated the dragons, they apparently didn't seem embarrassed at all. I was becoming more like a hero instead. It almost felt like the stronger I was, the more I could get away with.

"All right, let's keep going! Next up is Flatorte's uncle—Baldando, Baldando!"

"Aren't you prioritizing your relatives a little too much, Flatorte?!"

Well, whatever. All I had to do was square away these dragons. Everything was for Flatorte's sake—actually, I didn't know if it was anymore, but it was true that my only choice was to fight.

The battles went on and on, and I managed to get through fifty people.

I hadn't been thinking too carefully about it, but I knew from the analyst's comment: "We've finally gotten through fifty people!"

By the way, I wasn't really tired at all. Almost every match was finished with one hit. I couldn't OHKO effortlessly, but if I ran right at them and put all my weight into it, that was enough for a finishing blow.

"We're almost out of people for you to fight, I see. You've proven to us that your strength is real, Mistress."

Flatorte seemed even prouder than I was. *Don't forget you're the judge here.*

There were a few dragons I hadn't fought yet, but I could hear them saying that since so-and-so lost, they stood no chance. There was probably some bigwig among the blue dragons I'd defeated.

"I guess that's it. Great, my job's done now."

But—someone unexpected walked briskly into the opponents' waiting area.

It was Laika.

"Battle with me, Lady Azusa."

Laika was the very earnest type, not one to pull pranks. I knew right away that she was being serious.

And her face was dead serious, too.

"Can I ask why first?" I couldn't say anything until I knew that.

"I have been working diligently under you as your apprentice, Lady Azusa, in order to better myself. I would like to confirm the results of my hard work by battling with you."

This was getting way too heavy. I'd lived an easier life, though.

"I've been watching you work hard all this time, so I know. But you'd have to put in the effort for a hundred, two hundred years for it to mean anything, not just one or two."

I myself didn't know a way to improve in such a short amount of time anyway.

"Indeed. I do not think I've improved very quickly in a short amount of time. I do not believe I can win against you. I just want to fight you. Actually, I want to lose. I cannot keep moving forward unless I lose."

That was a very Laika-like thing to say. If she'd been thinking this hard about it, then I couldn't just brush her off.

"Sure. But in exchange, don't come crying to me if you get hurt. I'm guessing I'd be missing the point if I went easy on you for this fight."

"Thank you!" I could tell how passionate she was just by her voice.

"And so, Flatorte, keep acting as judge."

"Ah, very well… I hate to say this, but there's no reason for me to be a judge, is there? Your strength is the real deal, Mistress."

That might be. I didn't feel like budging on my victory, not even an inch. It would be an easy win for me.

"It'd be rude to Laika if this wasn't a proper match. I want you to announce the winner and loser like a real judge."

"O-okay!" Flatorte seemed to understand what I meant.

There came cheers from the watchers around us, but then it immediately went quiet.

Everyone wanted to see everything that happened.

The stakes were just that high, for both Laika and me.

She transformed into a magnificent red dragon.

Ahhh, I recalled when Laika had first come to challenge me to a fight.

Back then, I had wanted to thank her for coming.

Had I never met her, I don't think I ever would've thought of creating a family like we have now. It was a real hassle when she came, and my house got kind of wrecked, but in return, I received so much happiness.

Life was funny that way.

"I will give it everything I have."

"Of course you will. I would be angry if you gave less than a hundred percent after how much you've grown."

Flatorte looked between Laika and me, then she brought her raised hand down with a "B-begin!"

Laika flew up into the air to start then dove straight down at me, face-first.

I see. She was trying to get a hit in on me because slow, deliberate attacks like breathing flames wouldn't do anything.

Her hand moved slightly. So she was planning on tossing me away, huh?

If it connected, I'd be sent flying far into the distance.

And so instead of dodging it—I would let it land and stop it with all my strength!

I spread out my arms, like I was going to give a big hug, then clapped them shut to catch it.

I got a heavy shock, but I managed to stop it.

The shock was the first damage I'd taken all day.

Laika didn't say anything, either. We were battling, after all, and she was still concentrating.

I could sense her will. The only thing she lacked was force, and all she had to do about that was continue to improve under me.

"All right, and here's my counterattack."

I kicked and punched Laika over and over.

It was a boring attack, but each powerful hit chipped steadily away at Laika's strength.

And then, at last, I aimed for the sky—

And kicked her like a soccer ball into the air.

After a long hang time, Laika's dragon form crashed on a mountain just outside the village.

I could feel the ground shudder slightly all the way over from where I was.

A murmur immediately rippled through the crowd.

I glanced at Flatorte. "The verdict, Judge?"

"Oh, uhhh... Laika, Laika? Can you stand?"

From far away came a deep dragon voice: "I cannot..."

Flatorte came right over to me and raised her hand. "The winner is Mistress!"

After that, I was finally freed from fighting.

Well, I was caught in a flurry of questions from the blue dragons, so I wasn't really free yet... In a way, this part was more grueling than the fights.

In the meantime, Flatorte got some alone time with her family, so it was all okay. Sure, Flatorte would be alive for much longer than my three hundred years, but a daughter was still a daughter no matter how old she was.

On the other hand, Laika seemed a little glum.

"Hey, Laika, what's got you down?"

During a brief lull in the blue dragons' interrogation, I peeked at her from below, and Laika's face flushed in embarrassment.

"I am not down! I just... Now I realize what an absurd thing I asked of you. I'm so mortified..."

Right. So she couldn't look me in the eye.

I pressed her cheeks firmly between my hands.

"Wh-wha—!"

She couldn't speak well with her cheeks squished. Her face looked a little funny.

"You made a firm decision about what you wanted, so you have no reason to be embarrassed. Live with pride!"

"I—I unnershtan..."

As long as she got it. I let her go.

"You've gotten stronger, haven't you, Laika? I want you to keep improving."

I needed to follow up with my apprentices from time to time.

Laika's face immediately brightened.

"Thank you! I will devote myself to it!"

Laika's joining us on this trip was unexpected, but she still gained something from it.

You never knew what would happen in life—that was what made it interesting.

We reaped our own rewards from our trip to the blue dragon village.

But then, Laika's mouth started twitching, and—

"Ha*choo!*"

—she sneezed loudly.

"Lady Azusa, it's much too cold here..."

"Yeah, I agree with you..."

We shivered, breathing out white clouds.

Moving around in a fight was the perfect activity to stave off this cold.

I had a little chat with Flatorte on our way back to the house in the highlands.

"Did your parents understand? I'm not that worried, though, to be honest."

"Yes. They told me to serve the strongest witch with pride."

"That's it, huh? Well, just let me know if you want to go back again."

Home for me was the house in the highlands, but not for everyone else.

"Okay! If I do, please take me back! But if you come with me, you might be asked to fight everyone again, Mistress."

"Urgh… Then I may have to ask you to make it a once-in-a-while thing…"

The moment we got back to the house, we heard the sounds of the lute.

"The winters are colder when I'm all alone... ♪ I wrap myself in my blanket, and my heat keeps the cold away... ♪ Ohhh, I never knew that I could be the one to warm me up...♪"

Kuku's gloomy song echoed through the house… It sounded like a curse.

"Oh, Mommy…you're home…"

Falfa came up to me, but the skip in her step was gone and replaced with something heavier.

"It feels dark in here. Are you okay...? Oh no! Shalsha, what's wrong?!"

Farther into the room, Shalsha stood at an angle, her forehead pressed against the wall.

That's the first time I've seen anyone besides a drunk standing like that...

"Despair. I can't see the light. I can't feel anything. Pessimistic philosophy..."

"Shalsha! Shalsha! It's okay to mope, but please don't do it standing like that!" I hurriedly sat her in a chair.

While that was all happening, I could hear, "**It's just one of those Sundays, where it feels like everyone's laughing at me as they pass me by...** ♪" coming from Kuku's room.

"Lady Azusa, it seems everyone's fallen into despair after listening to these songs constantly."

"I see. I guess hearing these moody tunes has had an effect on Falfa and Shalsha."

But Flatorte had her arms crossed, and she seemed to be enjoying herself.

"Hmm. She's established her own sound. She's talking about the world in her own words."

It was a good song, sure. It had a power that melted into your heart—grabbed it and held it fast.

But, of course, having your heart in a tight grip wouldn't do much good for your spirit...

"Wait. How is everyone else doing...?"

"Halkara should be out working at the factory. I believe the effects would be minimal in that case."

There was logic to what Laika said, but when it came to Halkara, we should probably prepare for the worst.

We opened the door to Halkara's room.

There she was, sitting listlessly on her bed, still in her pajamas.

"Oh, I didn't want to go to work... I ended up skipping..."

"Halkara, what's wrong? What happened to you...?"

"I wish the world would go up in roaring flames... Just turn the elvish forests to ash..."

This was bad. Her eyes were dead. She didn't even want to go to work! Well, I knew the feeling of wanting to skip, but that was because my work life had been awful. Not the same thing.

"Here, first, stand up, and let's get you some water!"

"It's too much work to drink water..."

"Then let's get you some sunshine! It'll be good for you to be in the sun for at least twenty minutes!"

"It's too much work to go outside..."

This was a serious case. *Oh right, I know what we can do!*

I took a bottle of Nutri-Spirits and forced the contents down Halkara's throat.

Signs of life began to stir in her eyes. "Oh...I almost feel like doing things now..."

"Good! Your drink is super effective!"

"If we're talking about super effective, try Miss Kuku's songs. At first, I was pleasantly calmed, but after that, it felt like my soul was sinking into the ground."

Halkara told me what had happened, and I got the gist of it.

To put it simply, Kuku's talent had blossomed out of control.

They say that geniuses often sent the lives of those around them off course, and that was exactly the case here.

"But I'm glad you've recovered, Halkara. And next is...Rosalie..."

At the very least, she hadn't been floating in the dining room.

"Do you need me, Big Sis?" Rosalie popped out from the floor. I almost screamed.

"Um, can you appear more like a normal person next time...? Oh, you seem fine."

I didn't see the downer effect on her spirit.

"Oh, come on. When you're already dead, listening to the living cry about life is kiddie stuff. It's like hearing a five-year-old tell you about how hard life is! Ha-ha-ha!" Rosalie burst out laughing. "They can whine about how much pain they're in, but they haven't killed themselves, have they? I already killed myself! And I was an evil spirit, remember? Bah-ha-ha! Against that, their problems can't even register as pain!"

"I can't tell if that's a good thing or a bad thing!"

Afterward, I told Kuku to practice outside during the day.

"I'm sorry. I thought I could get better..."

She seemed to finally notice when I told her, and she ended up feeling guilty.

"Oh, I know how you feel. Still, please practice outside."

"But when I'm in the sun, my mood vastly improves, so it's not very suited to my practice... It is a dark song, after all..."

That's the problem!

But then I came up with a great idea.

"So you'd prefer somewhere dark?"

"Yes. Terribly dark and gloomy would be perfect."

"In that case, we have a cellar that we use to store food, so can you do that in there?"

After she gave it a go, she sang its praises. "The acoustics are very good. It's fantastic." Oh, right. The dark underground was kind of like a live music club.

After that, Kuku spent a long time practicing in the cellar.

The day finally came for us to go to the music festival.

And, as always, an enormous creature flew through the sky and straight for us. Kuku was shocked, but we were used to it.

It was a leviathan—Vania, judging by her color.

After a moment, Fatla stepped down.

"You are all invited as national guests. Please step on board."

"Thank you, as always, Fatla."

"Oh, no, this is my job. Incidentally, Lady Beelzebub is at a meeting and thus not present. She was terribly sad that she could not travel with the girls. She even cried."

Maybe I was being too sensitive, but I couldn't get over how she said *the girls*. Was Beelzebub starting to think of Falfa and Shalsha as her own...?

We climbed aboard Vania and received the same instructions as we did before.

"We've added a new building since last time, so we will show you around."

Huh? What for?

We went inside, and there was Fighsly the Fighter Slime, punching a round object hanging from the ceiling.

Placed around the room were several apparatuses that were either for training or torture—it was hard to tell.

"This is the training room. Fighsly is using it today."

"Oh, hello, everyone! I am practicing to master Fighsly-style slime fist! Would you like to join me?"

"...I'm all right."

But Laika chimed in: "I will work up a sweat here!"

Afterward, we hung around a sort of lounge.

Kuku sat still for a while, but she finally stood up.

"I...am going to practice... I cannot keep calm..."

"I guess that's what happens when you go onstage. Practice all you need until you shake off those jitters."

The rest of us flipped through the music festival programs scattered around the lounge (translated from the demon language for our convenience).

The festival would take place over three days.

The venues would be all over the area outside Vanzeld Castle, and the four biggest stages were in the stadium, at the burial grounds, in the field at the old execution grounds, and in the reclaimed miasma swamp.

It was almost like a regular music festival, but the locations of the stages were a little eerie.

"According to the book that Beelzebub gave me before, there were once many executions on celebration days when they partied extensively. This is a holdover from that," the knowledgeable Shalsha told me.

"I see… Were they like sacrifices, I wonder?"

"They say these celebrations had parades and plenty of pop-up shops. It was very lively."

"Huh. Well, given it's the demons putting this on, I imagine it'll be over-the-top."

Kuku would perform on the second day at the burial grounds. Most of the audience would be standing, but there were seats in the back. Wait, the seats looked like gravestones…

"And then on the last day, the demon king comes out to the stadium and renews her contract with the god of sound to control that sound, and that's the end. It was originally a religious affair."

"Maybe these kinds of festivals originate from religion no matter what world you're in."

Just then, Fatla came in with honey water. She sure worked hard.

"In general, please think of this as a festival with musical elements. We would like you to participate as our honored guests at the event in which the demon king will perform on the last day, but you are free to do as you please otherwise."

"Then we should take a look around the castle town on the first day. There's a place I want to visit."

"And where might that be?" Fatla seemed surprised that I had a destination in mind.

"Remember? Pondeli should be living in the castle town. I was thinking about paying her a quick visit."

Pondeli was a catperson who had died from hunger and turned into an undead.

She should be operating a game lounge in Vanzeld town.

I was the one who came up with that idea. She had been out of employment, education, or training for a long time, so I suggested a job even she could do: playing games with other people.

I'd played a big role in her life, so I felt obligated to check in on her. And I also wanted to make sure she was actually working... She was practically a hard-core NEET, after all...

"Miss Pondeli is working hard. She's consistently paying her resident tax, at least."

"That's your standard?"

She must be doing well enough if she was making enough money to pay her taxes.

"But this is going to be such a lively festival, perhaps I should've established a stall for Halkara Pharmaceuticals."

As always, Halkara was a salesperson raring to go. Her moxie had carried her through life.

"Indeed. There are companies from all over setting up shop to advertise. This year, you should observe to see if it is viable for you, then submit an application to open a booth next time."

"Yes, understood!"

"Incidentally, applications for booths will be on sale at the venue this year, and we will be accepting applications for next time the day after the music festival is over. There is a high chance you will be rejected if your paperwork is not in order, so please check what you fill in very carefully."

It felt like rules from a fan convention were applied to all sorts of things in this world. Well, I guess clerical work was the same everywhere...

"Additionally, if you would like to come in costume, you will need proof of permission to dress up, so be sure to apply for that, too."

This is *a convention!*

Maybe fan culture is universal. I bet that's it.

A little while later, both Kuku and Laika came back, dripping with sweat.

"I got some great practice." (Kuku)

"I got some great practice." (Laika)

I hadn't thought they'd both say the exact same thing. They were practicing completely different things, though.

Kuku's expressions suggested she did everything she'd wanted to do. Her rabbit ears seemed to be standing more upright than usual.

Fighsly swung by later, and Laika had a cheery chat with her.

"Fighsly-style slime fist is rather complex. I believe I can become more efficient should I adopt parts of it."

"Yes. Efficiency is a key element of Fighsly style, after all."

"I will use it to defeat many slimes!"

"Yes, please do!"

Really? Telling someone who used to be a slime that you're going to defeat slimes...? But Fighsly herself didn't seem to mind...

We feasted on Fatla's delicious cooking that day as we headed for the castle. Both of the leviathan sisters were great at cooking.

The next morning, Vania landed near the castle without incident.

Early as it was, some shops were already open in the castle town, and there were more people around than before. From there, we went into the castle.

As when we came to receive the Demon Medal, we were taken to the guest room, and after that, we were left to our own devices.

"Miss Kuku, you're free to do what you like today, but you are welcome to get an initial look at your venue and do a sound check. What do you think?" Fatla asked after showing us to our room.

"I will go, of course. It's the biggest stage I'll have ever been on..."

There was nothing to worry about.

"You have it all together, don't you, Kuku?" I asked.

"Yes!" she responded enthusiastically.

So that meant the rest of us would take a stroll around the festival. Fatla gave us a map of the castle town.

Fighsly invited me to the gym, but I respectfully declined. You don't really need to go to the gym on a festival day, do you?

Every street was crowded with people. There were stalls on either side, so the roads were narrower than usual, and with the throngs of people, everything was a mess.

"Finding Pondeli's shop isn't going to be easy..."

I was looking at the map of the castle town that Fatla gave us, but the distances were farther than I imagined, and there were some places where the roads were so intertwined that it was hard to tell them apart.

But even in Japan, game shops were usually in out-of-the-way places, so there wasn't much I could do about that. People who weren't into that stuff never needed to step inside, and for nerds, they'd want to go even if it meant having to search for it, so the difficulty finding it wouldn't pose too much of a problem.

Incidentally, Rosalie seemed displeased by how the people walking on the streets kept passing through her.

There were lots of demons who could see her, but it was so crowded that they had to go through her anyway. She probably felt unsettled having people do that to her.

And she wasn't the only unhappy member of our group.

"Waaah, it's too crowded..."

"If you clear your mind, even the hottest fires will feel cool, Big Sister."

Shalsha, that basically just means "deal with it." Actually, I didn't know that saying existed in this world, too...

But it would be bad if the two little ones got separated from me and got lost. I needed to think of a way to prevent that.

"Hey, Laika? Is there a way to keep us from losing Falfa and Shalsha?"

"Lady Azusa, we lost Halkara."

The question got me a missing persons report!

"W-well... She knows where we're going, and she also has a map, so I think we could probably reconvene with her... Wow, she really is lost..."

There were no cell phones in this world, so it was going to be hard to meet up now that we were separated.

"Laika, what should we do to make sure the two don't end up like Halkara?"

"I believe holding hands is the most reliable way."

That might be true, but it was way too crowded. Holding hands and making space for ourselves to walk abreast would just make us an obstacle for everyone else...

"Oooh, oooh! Falfa wants to ride on Mommy's shoulders!" Falfa said almost instantly.

Oh, that was a great idea! That way, she could also see the festival around us.

But that brought up another problem: There was only one of me...

"Shalsha is the younger sister, so I take priority. I insist that I ride on Mom's shoulders," Shalsha said, as though it was clearly obvious.

Right—I couldn't carry them both on my shoulders at the same time.

"Awww, why does the littler sister get priority?" Falfa objected.

"Because you're supposed to spoil little sisters."

"That's stupid. Because you could fall when you're up on someone's shoulders. That's why your big sister, Falfa, should do it. It's for your sake, Shalsha."

Falfa was putting her foot down, but I smelled a lie!

This would just become an endless argument. I had to put an end to the conversation.

"Okay, Mommy's going to make the decision. Falfa's the one who came up with the idea, so she's going to ride on my shoulders."

"Yaaay! I won the case!"

That was a weird way to be happy about it.

But then, of course, Shalsha pouted. She looked like she was going to cry. Even the most sensible girl would want to shed a tear or two in this situation. And sometimes, seeing those childlike parts of her was a relief for her mom.

And I wasn't planning on leaving it at that, of course.

"I want to appeal to a higher court…"

"Shalsha, you can ride on the shoulders of one of your other big sisters."

I shifted my gaze to Flatorte. She was taller than Laika, after all.

Flatorte seemed to understand what I wanted, and she gave a thumbs-up as a signal to leave it to her.

Shalsha went over to her and bowed her head. "Thank you."

"Of course! Leave it to me, Flatorte!"

She immediately squatted down, ready for Shalsha to climb on.

"But, Shalsha? Don't touch my horns… It wouldn't be good if I started having to obey everything you said…"

Oh, right, that could be a problem… *Did I pick the wrong person…? Maybe I should've picked Laika…*

"I almost did. They're so easy to hold on to."

"Oh, Shalsha, seriously, be careful! This is a very delicate problem!"

Anyway, the two were happy to ride on our shoulders.

"Wooow! There are so many people!"

"I feel like a giant. Even the smallest human riding on the shoulders of a titan will have a wide field of vision."

Good, they're having fun. That's practically a child's job.

And then, we heard our errant Halkara's voice.

"Madam Teacher!!! Where are you?! Please answer me!!!"

It looked like we could reconvene without any problems. When we met up, Halkara was on the verge of tears.

"Oh, Madam Teacher… I was all alone in this foreign land. I was so sad…"

I thought my daughters were going to be the ones to cry, not Halkara…

"Aren't you the type to live a good life on your own?"

"But I have a family now, don't I…?"

Well, that was a nice thing to hear, so I patted her head.

As we made for Pondeli's shop, we ended up getting to see all sorts of different stores. We had to walk quite a bit.

"I see. It seems like we could make quite a bit of money, even with a stall all the way out here. It's not terrible."

Halkara was the only one looking at things with a more unique perspective. She was serious about that booth.

"In fact, I think it might be possible to open three stores or so. It's just too good to put out only one. But placing it right in front of a large venue is also a possibility."

"You really have it together when it comes to stuff like this, don't you?"

"I am just happy to make money. And Halkara Pharmaceuticals doesn't have any competitors at the moment, either. I may as well build a factory in the demon lands!"

Not having any competitors was a big advantage.

Next to me, Flatorte looked like she was about to fall over.

Well, more like Shalsha, who was riding on her shoulders, was off-balance.

"I got so scared, I almost grabbed your horns."

"Ohhh, please don't do that! If you grab on tight with your legs, you won't fall, okay?!"

I felt bad for Flatorte. I'd done this to her... Still, Falfa had been having a ball, laughing and smiling this whole time.

As we made our way through, we reached an exceptionally crowded corner.

I could hear what sounded like a hawker.

"Oooh, what's over there; what's over there?! Falfa's super-duper-extra excited!"

I heard Falfa's voice coming from above me. The odd phrasing was okay because she was a kid. I don't know how I'd feel if I heard an adult say that.

"Okeydoke, then, we'll go over there."

"Yay! I love you, Mommy!"

Well! She told me she loved me. I wanted to wake up every morning hearing that.

"Miss Flatorte, we'll be going over there. Keep up with my big sister."

"It feels like we're playing horse…Very well…"

She's putting you to good use, Flatorte. You're doing great.

As we got closer, I realized why there was such a crowd.

There were so many banners advertising Mandragora pills!

And at the front of the store was a familiar redheaded witch.

"Today, I, Eno, renowned Witch of the Grotto, am here to personally sell you Mandragora pills! These are your greatest daily-use pills, sumptuously made from high-quality mandragoras! Our family doctor, Mandragora pills!"

She looked like she was having *so* much fun selling them!

"Buy one bottle today and get another one free! No price change! These are pills, so they will keep if you store them in a dry place! Feel free to buy as many as you like!"

Wow.

I'd thought about it before, but this girl was really animated when it came to customer-facing jobs…

"Well, if it isn't my senior, the great Witch of the Highlands!"

Eno seemed to have noticed us.

"Your business looks like it's going well. I'm happy to see a younger witch succeed."

"Yes. I know I'll make it big with this! See, as long as I'm alive, I want to win!"

"Oh yeah… I guess if that's what's right for you…"

This girl originally wanted to be a witch available only to those in the know, but once her product started selling, she sure changed her tune. Now she was thinking about how to sell even more…

"Oh yes, we also have kids' Mandragora pills for children. How about one?"

Eno brought out a different product. She sure was aggressive.

"I'll have to carry it around if I buy it now, so no thank you…"

After that, Eno greeted the rest of my family, and my daughters gave their polite hellos, too. Good.

But Halkara wore the expression of one facing a dangerous foe.

She sure is on alert... "What's wrong with you, Halkara?"

"I have a feeling that she could pose a threat to my business... This is a merchant's hunch..."

And her hunch was right.

This time, Eno pulled out a bottle of pale-yellow liquid.

"And today I've brought a new product—Forest Elixir! Forest Elixir is perfect for your nutritional supplements! It is chock-full of various herbs and mushrooms! Dilute one bottle with water every day and drink up! Forest Elixir will make you healthy from the inside out!"

Halkara went pale.

"Everyone, I know something we'll call N-S from a company we'll call HP has been selling recently, but treating fatigue with an energy drink is not good for you! You will not recover by temporarily forgetting about your exhaustion! Forest Elixir builds up your immune system slowly, over time, and raises your very status! Think about your health, and choose Forest Elixir!"

Uh-oh, I know what this is... A showdown between a nutritional supplement and a daily health drink...

"Wait, wait, wait! Do not defame my company!" Halkara leaped forward—she wouldn't stand for this!

"I didn't say Nutri-Spirits from Halkara Pharmaceuticals, though."

"You *basically* did! And there are no harmful components in Nutri-Spirits! Please do not say that it is bad for your health!"

"Is that so? But it's too hard on your body to drink every day."

"That's because it's meant for people who need extra energy to work at specific times! Don't you think it's weird to decry a product for a different use?!"

"Miss Halkara, was it? I don't admire the image you have of a worker gulping down a bottle. If it has ingredients that are supposed to have an effect right away, it has to be bad for you! You should not drink it to go for another round at work!"

"What about you, Miss Witch of the Grotto? If you need to drink that every day, then you may as well go for nutritionally balanced meals

©Benio

every day, and that's much healthier for you! Making people think that they're safe just drinking that every day is practically fraud!"

Oh no—this was going to be a more intense battle than I thought…

But the demons around them were urging them on, yelling, "More!" Was this a show now?!

And Falfa was also cheering. "You can do it, Big Sis Halkara!" *Falfa, this isn't a thing you should be cheering for…*

And then, two very strong and scary-looking Minotaur security guards came over.

"Hey, we heard there's a fight going on over here."

This time, both Eno and Halkara blanched.

"Oh, what are you talking about…? My shop is operating as per usual…"

"I am not entirely sure, either… I'm just an elf tourist…"

They sure were quick to act like they didn't know anything…

Halkara practically fled the scene. Actually, it looked like that's exactly what she did.

If we just let her be, she'd get lost again, so we followed her.

"Oh dear… I didn't think Halkara Pharmaceuticals would have a rival…"

"Sounds like a pickle, doesn't it?"

"In that case, I think my only choice is to start selling True Nutri-Spirits, Nutri-Spirits Relaxation, and Nutri-Power-Up-Spirits, which all use more valuable herbs, and pressure her with variety…"

Now that I thought about it, I never knew why there were so many different kinds of energy drinks on sale in Japan… Some went from dirt cheap to exceedingly expensive, so I really wondered if there was much difference among them.

I guess every world was destined for the same fate.

As we talked about all that, we carried on searching for Pondeli's shop.

"By the way, Lady Azusa, what sort of person is this Pondeli?" Laika asked.

None of them had met her before.

"To sum her up in a single sentence, she plays games like a girl possessed. Except she's already given up the ghost. She's an undead catperson who will literally play all day long."

"That seems to be quite an idle life. I'm not impressed."

It certainly was incompatible with Laika's values.

"Oh, there were plenty of people who hung out like that in the blue dragon village. While we were there, I spotted a few who started drinking before the sun went down and kept going until noon the next day. There was an older one sprawled out on the floor asleep."

After seeing the blue dragon village for myself, I couldn't even call that an exaggeration.

Still, I thought we had different definitions of "hanging out."

The one thing they all had in common, though, was that they weren't really doing any work...

"An undead, you say? I wonder who has the better lifestyle, an undead or a ghost?" Rosalie posed a question that was difficult for me to answer.

Plus, I had a hard time ignoring her choice of the word *life*style.

"You decide. We're not ghosts or undead, so we don't know..."

As we walked toward the outskirts of the castle town, the crowds finally started thinning.

And since there was no risk of getting lost anymore, the shoulder rides concluded.

"We just need to go straight down this road. Phew, we're almost there."

This town was massive. The shop was in an inconvenient spot, but it was pretty big. Maybe it used to be an assembly hall or something.

I opened the door, and along the many rows of tables, most of the demons there sat in twos, facing each other with serious looks.

Let's take a peek at the goblin and kobold nearby to see what they're doing.

"I summon Vengeful Centaur!" (Goblin)

"Then I'll summon King of the Sea Serpents and buff it with Water Plumes! After that, I'll make it un-block-able with the ability from Patron of Darkness, and then I'll attack!" (Kobold)

It was a card game!

It looked like everyone was playing the same game at every table.

"What is this…?"

And at the far end of the shop, Pondeli was sitting in what I assumed was the seat of the manager.

"It's been a while. It looks like you've been hard at work."

"Oh, Miss Azusa! You helped me a great deal before!"

Pondeli's cat tail was twitching back and forth. She appeared to have adjusted to this place now.

"Afterward, I thought just playing games regularly would be kind of boring, so I used what I learned from all the games I've played before to produce the greatest card game I've ever come up with. I brought the idea to a company in town, and they hired me, luckily."

"The demons are really advanced when it comes to this stuff…"

"It's the card game that everyone's playing now—Ket Keto."

Pondeli pulled out a box and bag that looked like merchandise.

"This is a starter box containing sixty cards, and this bag is a booster pack with fifteen."

I sometimes wondered if the people on this world came from Earth.

"The number of players is blowing up. I'm very busy right now because I have to decide on the setting for the next round of booster packs. I have to basically lock myself in my room and check the game balance over and over again."

Holing up in her room was exactly what she did before, but she seemed to be having so much fun, and her eyes were sparkling. I could've sworn I saw more color in her face, too.

Ahhh, now I see the trick.

People at risk of becoming shut-ins could still find jobs where they could work.

"Congratulations. This is all great, Pondeli."

"What? I just came up with a game I thought would be fun. I'm still doing the same thing I did in the graveyard."

Pondeli herself didn't seem aware of it, though.

I wondered if Pondeli's history as a NEET was what gave her such a knack for this. If so, then maybe it was all for a reason. Meat was tastier aged, after all.

As she watched on, Laika also murmured her honest opinion: "What a lovely sight."

"Shalsha wants to play this game. I'm interested."

All right. I knew if Shalsha put her heart into it, she'd become the champion in no time. #biasedmom

After I met Pondeli, I had bought several games for my daughters to play, and they became obsessed with one of those card games. Of course she'd be interested to see a new one.

"In that case, shall I gift you a few cards?"

"It's fine; we'll buy them."

I bought a rule book just for Shalsha. I knew it would get insanely expensive if she got obsessed, but this was just intellectual training! No problems here!

Just then, one of the tables seemed to come to the end of their game, and the winner brought the match results to the operations table.

We may as well watch from behind the table.

"Oh, Barunda has five straight wins, and so does Keika. Our finals match might be between two undefeated parties."

The other players must have heard, because they started getting excited.

"Is it Barunda's aggro deck, like they say?" "No, Keika's Happy Central Drake is strong. Aggressiveness is barely even a threat." "I think the sideboarding after the first game will be key here."

Some people were pretty into it. The beginnings of this card game were going well.

"Since it is the finals, why don't we do our sixth match first so these people may watch. Any objections?"

There was some applause in response to Pondeli's idea.

Wow, she was pretty good at winging it, too!

And we could watch the finals match ourselves.

The finals would take place on the center table, where it was easiest to watch.

Barunda was an older, muscular orc.

On the other side of the table was Keika, a mini demon wearing a hat. He still seemed young.

"Boy, this will make you a man."

"I'm young, so I've had plenty of time to dedicate to this. Get ready for a shutout."

"You know what this table means, right?"

"Of course. What do you think this arena is used for?"

Oooh, sparks are flying before the match even starts! Incredible! Literally—there was a flame spirit or something in the audience. *Get a hold of yourself; this is dangerous!*

And so the match between the orc and the mini demon began.

"Hey, Pondeli? I don't really understand this. Could you explain?"

"Sure, of course."

Her tail was casually waving back and forth, and I wanted to grab it. She'd probably get mad at me if I did, though.

"First, the cards are mainly divided into energy cards and magic cards. You need energy cards to use magic cards. Energy cards will first come out during the initial phases, so it might be a little uneventful, but the aggressive deck will attack during these phases."

I see.

"And he summons Lightning Spirit! This card can attack during the same turn it comes on to the battlefield, so here he goes!"

Oooh, the orc suddenly summoned something and attacked.

The mini demon couldn't guard, so he took damage.

"Eeeeeeee!" the mini demon cried. It was like he himself was being shocked!

"Hey, how does this work?"

"When you take damage at this battle table, the corresponding damage goes straight to the player. I've drawn a special magic circle on the floor."

"It's more dangerous than I thought..."

I trusted she had proper safety measures in place, though...

"And people's clothes often rip as a result of the damage, so the male players get very excited when female players come."

"Don't force them into something sexual!"

The orc was bringing out monsters one after the other during his opening move and attacking with them.

On the other hand, the mini demon was strengthening his defenses with some kind of wall.

But the orc's attacks were breaking through the barriers in accordance with some rule or another I didn't really understand and dealing damage to the mini demon.

"Aaaaagh! Rrrgh!"

Flames and lightning were bursting from below the mini demon, and he was getting pretty beaten up. In a way, it was a game suitable for demons, but it was cruel...

"Wait, this is strange... Madam Teacher, don't you think it's odd?" Halkara sounded like she had discovered something. "Doesn't that mini-demon boy have something of a chest?"

It was just as the orc was about to use an attack spell to deal the finishing blow.

"It looks like this victory is mine, boy. It's risky to wait too long before you make your move."

"Heh. Unfortunately, you won't be able to use that." Keika the mini demon grinned.

Wait, could this be when he starts on his comeback?! That'll get me all fired up, too!

Keika hid his chest, and then threw off his hat.

Shoulder-length hair fell from inside it.

"I'm not a boy but a girl! If you use that magic attack, my clothes will be torn to shreds!"

Keika wasn't a young man but a young lady!

"Dammit! This is foul play! Card games are a gentleman's sport! If I attack you any more, they'll think I did it to see you naked!" The orc was in anguish.

"That's right! That means you can't put an end to this match!" Keika cried, elated at her success. Was this against the rules?!

"Ohhh! This development is getting me excited!" "She's using the really-a-girl trick, after all this time!" "We got the psychological warfare at the last minute!"

The peanut gallery all seemed fine with it. *Is this okay? I mean, like, in general? This has nothing to do with cards at this point, right?*

"Well, well! This final match is really heating up!"

Pondeli seemed extremely pleased. The sponsor herself was okay with this. Maybe I was the only one who wasn't…

"Miss Azusa, the game doesn't just happen on the table. Shaking your opponent psychologically to attack is also a splendid strategy."

"You make it sound really important, but I don't buy it."

"One time, a player set the building on fire to force his opponent to run away and abandon the match in a tournament."

"You should just fight with the cards."

"Also, that person was arrested."

And they lost way too much for a victory.

"Speaking of fighting with cards, there are some players who throw the cards around like knives and stab them into their enemy's arms."

"Don't use the cards physically!"

Demon card games were much too dark.

On the other hand, the strange tactics on the battlefield were still going strong.

"Heh-heh, if I move my hand while I'm drawing a card, you might see my chest."

"Stop! Don't tempt me after you've already dealt me intermediate damage!"

"Now, why don't you use that attacking magic of yours and have everyone recognize you as a pervert? Or maybe you'll sit there and take it when I summon this Highly Attentive but Unable to Act Accordingly Drake?"

Keika's strategy might come out on top here, but I wasn't totally sold on the methods when she looked like a fifth grader.

But in the midst of this insidious reversal, the orc drew a card.

At that moment, his expression changed.

"God has smiled on me during this match today."

"Wh-what? That's impossible... You couldn't defeat me without dealing damage to me..."

"But there is such magic! I use Otherworldly Summon! I can use one thing here in this arena!"

I was doubtful of this card.

The orc slowly stood from his seat and ripped the curtain from the window.

To top it off, he threw it onto Keika.

"Ahhh! I can't see!"

"If you're completely covered, then I can attack as much as I want! Here I'll use An Insanely Crazy Inferno! You take two thousand damage!"

"Ahhhhhh! Raaaaagh!" I could hear her voice coming from inside the curtain, and Keika then fell over.

Pondeli rushed over to the space and announced, "Barunda is the winner!"

As cheers erupted in the arena, my family and I looked on in astonishment.

It was nothing like the card game I imagined...

"And here we present the winner, Barunda, with a limited-edition card—Azusa, Witch of the Highlands."

©Benio

She handed him a card that violated my personality rights! You could even see my panties in the illustration!

I patted Shalsha on the shoulder.

"This card game is bad for your upbringing, so you can't play it."

Shalsha seemed a little disappointed, but she nodded.

Now that we'd seen Pondeli again, we returned to the room we were staying in.

A little while afterward, Kuku finished her practice and came into our room.

"I did everything I could. Now I just wait for tomorrow."

Kuku seemed satisfied, so it didn't look like there was anything for me to be worried about.

"Sometimes, you just have to fight. Break a leg."

"Oh, and these are tickets for related parties. I have enough for everyone."

Getting these for us meant she was treating us like family. The demons were really considerate when it came to stuff like this.

But that didn't mean Kuku was family.

She'd written plenty of new songs, so she would have to go back to the royal capital to resume her activities.

That was why this music festival would be our good-bye to Kuku.

I wasn't *not* sad about it, but I couldn't force her to stay. I gripped the tickets tightly with both my hands.

"Got it. Make those demons bawl with your music!"

That night, we went to bed a little earlier than usual out of consideration for what Kuku had to do the next day. Even though this was a guest bed, it was huge. There were some demons who were really big, so maybe they made it big enough for them.

Suddenly, I sensed someone standing by my pillow and opened my eyes.

It was Kuku.

"Um… I suddenly got really anxious… Would it be all right to sleep in the same bed as you, just for today…?"

I smiled and slid to the side.

"Go ahead. I want you to be in tip-top shape."

It was sort of funny to see her adjusting her rabbit ears as she slept.

FLATORTE

A blue dragon girl who obeys what Azusa says. Since she's a dragon like Laika, there is somewhat of a rivalry between them, but she's an optimistic and energetic girl. Unlike Laika, she has a tail in human form.

ROSALIE

A ghost girl and resident of the house in the highlands. She's devoted to Azusa, who didn't shy away from her as a ghost and instead reached out to her. She can go through walls but can't touch people. She can also possess others.

PECORA
(PROVATO PECORA ARIÉS)

The demon king. A girl with a devilish temperament who loves to use her power and influence to bewilder her subordinates and Azusa. She actually has a masochistic desire to be subordinate to someone stronger than she is, and she adores Azusa.

And so, day two of the music festival.

Kuku went ahead to the venue first, and the rest of the family took our time getting to the stage at the burial grounds.

We handed over our tickets and went inside, and sure enough, there was a row of gravestones-turned-seats with a good view of the stage. I guess that was where we would be watching from. It was a cursed spot, but maybe it was fine for demons.

An artist was already performing, and the demon fans were cheering.

After a little while, the leviathan sisters Fatla and Vania, Fighsly, and even Beelzebub came over.

"These are our seats, no?"

Oh right, the seats beside me were empty—must have been Beelzebub's.

"Work has finally calmed down. They made me man the booth for bizarre-yet-delicious vegetables created from selective breeding."

Beelzebub was fanning herself. That sounded like something the agricultural minister would do.

"Kuku isn't known at all among the demons. I'm still a little worried about that…"

Even if the venue was packed, she would have a hard time if they treated her like an away team. I hoped it wouldn't cause her lifelong trauma… That was the one reservation I couldn't let go of until it was all over.

"You fool. The audience recognizes that one must be recognized as a skilled performer to be allowed to stand on the biggest stages of the music festival. They will listen carefully."

All I could do was believe Beelzebub for now.

"I just gave her the opportunity. It is she who decides if she will seize it. It's on her shoulders to choose whether she will succeed in leaving a good impression on a large audience or fail."

"It sounds like you're distancing yourself from her, but you're right."

All we could do was watch.

Falfa and Laika folded their hands naturally, like they were praying.

On the other hand, Flatorte seemed relaxed as she sipped a drink while she waited.

Actually, she might have only appeared calmer than she was.

"Becoming too familiar with a minstrel will make me attached, and that's no good. If I begin to worry about their personal lives, I can no longer be as nerdy as I have been until now."

That sounded like something that someone who was in too deep would say. Maybe she was right.

Kuku's turn was approaching slowly.

The one who performed before her was a fat troll who was apparently an opera singer and certainly had the voice of one.

And then, it was Kuku's turn.

The MC introduced her: "Miss Kuku is a novice almiraj, one who has recently had a vast change in genre." She wasn't a novice in terms of her career, but this *was* her first performance in her new genre.

"I can't sit still, so I'm going to float up and look from above!"

Rosalie left her seat and drifted upward.

Kuku finally appeared from offstage.

There was a strap attached to her lute so that it hung from her shoulder. She was the picture of a singer-songwriter.

"I'm Kuku. My first song is called 'Thank You.'"
Then she began to play a somber yet gentle melody on her lute.

It's time~ It's too sad to have to say good-bye~
So I'll say instead, thank you~ ♪

I hadn't heard her practicing this song at the house before.
But when I heard the lyrics, I could tell right away.
This song was for us.

I won't be gone forever; I'm just moving somewhere else~
We'll live on in our separate places, live on in our own times~
And we may forget each other, 'cause that's just part of life~
But part of life is remembering, too~
So it's okay, no surprises, come and see me anytime~
Thank you, thank you, thank you~ ♪

When the first song was over, I stood up and applauded, tears running down my face.
"You did it, Kuku!"
My daughters followed suit and stood up, too. And it wasn't just us; so many members of the demon audience were giving her a standing ovation.
Among them all, only Flatorte stayed sitting, pressing her hands against her eyes and sobbing quietly.
It was like a master looking on as a disciple reached greatness.
Kuku's songs were amazing, and they touched our hearts. They didn't always have to be dark.
In the end, Kuku played seventeen songs, left the stage for a moment, was hastily brought back onstage to the fervent calls for an encore, played another three songs, and then it was finally over.
"Here, a new handkerchief. I have plenty, so pass it on."
Beelzebub sure did have a lot of handkerchiefs.
Now that she mentioned it, I noticed we were all crying.

That night, I immediately grabbed Kuku into a hug when we reunited.

"You did it! You were incredible! Everyone was cheering for you!"

"Thank you so much! I never thought it'd go this well..." Tears rolled down Kuku's face as she smiled. "This is all thanks to you. I have no idea how I can tell you how grateful I am..."

"What? There's only one thing to say," I replied as I recalled Kuku's performance. "And that's *thank you*, right?"

Kuku beamed and said, "Thank you!" and hugged me again, and I gently stroked the backs of her ears.

That day, thanks to Beelzebub's kindness, we had one of the rooms in the castle prepared for us for a celebration party.

Plates of food just kept coming in—it was a huge feast.

Kuku's expression was also bright. I mean, that was a given after her performance went off without a hitch.

"Interested parties from various venues who saw you sing today have already sent in mounds of requests. Here is a quick list of all of them, Kuku."

I couldn't really read demonic script, but I could see that she had tons of work coming in.

"Is this...enough work to live in the castle town here...?" Kuku looked at the list, astonished.

She'd probably never had requests like this before.

"Perhaps. Well, you used to live in the human capital, so why don't you see if you can make a living there as you take on a healthy amount of work. I can lend you a wyvern for transport, so it wouldn't be impossible to do both at the same time."

"That's great, Kuku. You're suddenly a hit! This means you were a big hit with the demons!"

But Kuku didn't seem to be honestly happy yet—maybe because it didn't feel real to her.

All these happenings were such a sudden change, so I understood.

Our feast continued, and the mood was peaceful from beginning to end. Halkara was already passed-out drunk, and Falfa and Shalsha were already asleep from exhaustion.

Vania laughed at Halkara for being drunk, then passed out herself fifteen minutes later.

Her older sister, Fatla, was irritated. "She never learns..."

Flatorte had barely had any water, but she was barely talking to Kuku, either.

Of course, I could tell, because I was keeping a careful eye on my family.

But I wasn't sure how to approach the subject, so I just watched.

Flatorte appeared to be dealing with some sort of conflict that the rest of the family wasn't.

If she wasn't, she would have been having more fun or been sadder about Kuku leaving.

And then, just as the feast was about to come to an end—

Flatorte asked Kuku, "Can I borrow your lute?"

"Yes, sure."

It was a precious tool of her trade, but Kuku allowed it. Flatorte had an oddly cryptic look on her face, but I doubted she was going to do something she shouldn't because she was drunk.

"Are you going to sing a parting song?" Laika asked.

As a fellow dragon, Laika was probably worried about Flatorte.

"Not quite," Flatorte said, and she stood right in front of Kuku. "I have one song for you. It's not very good, though."

Then she began to play—

"WOOOOOOOAAAAAAAAH, DESTRUCTION, DESTRUCTION, DESTRUCTION! WOOOOAAAAAAAAHHHHH, EXECUTION, EXECUTION, EXECUTION!"

This was one of Schifanoia's songs!

But Flatorte was a better singer than Schifanoia, so her performance had a bit more flavor. I didn't know if I should be pleased, though.

©Benio

Flatorte's mouth and eyes were opened wide as sound poured out of her. "Schifanoia! In the past, you've sung as Schifanoia so much that you even knocked yourself unconscious. It may not sell, but that's because you believed it was right, so if you ever want to go back, then you should. Don't be an idiot and think you *have* to seal it away forever! You aren't smart enough to follow what's popular in society! If you were, you would've sold out ages ago!"

Flatorte's loud voice echoed in the room.

"Even I, Flatorte, have made mistake after mistake, and I found myself here. There might not be a right answer, but as long as you keep going, you'll never totally fail! So sing how you want! It's your life!"

Flatorte then thrust the lute out to Kuku.

Kuku gripped it tightly.

"You *are* master and pupil," I murmured, and Laika and Beelzebub beside me nodded.

"This is something the master can tell the pupil all because she's made her mistakes."

Laika watched the two with a refreshing smile.

Flatorte's grown a lot, too. People could change by meeting others.

"It's because of you that this could happen, and it's all right to be proud of that. I perhaps wouldn't have reacted this way without you," Beelzebub said as she poured me another glass of alcohol.

"This is strong, so please don't give me too much..."

"It's fine. The demon king's performance at the festival tomorrow is in the evening."

Oh right, we had to see Pecora perform, since we were national guests.

"What is she going to do? Is she going to raise a lit torch or something? Or give a closing address?"

Beelzebub smiled bitterly and muttered, "You'll see."

What was going to happen now...? The demon king had to do *something...*

The next day, Laika apparently woke up early to train with Fighsly. She sure was a hard worker, even in the morning...

Falfa and Shalsha both said they'd gone to the library to read some books. They must have woken up early, since they fell asleep during dinner.

Everyone else—besides Rosalie, who didn't need sleep, being a ghost and all—slept for so long it could be counted as sleeping in. Even me.

"You're finally up, Big Sis."

Rosalie startled me when I opened my eyes, hovering right in front of me.

"You could've woken me up earlier, Rosalie..."

"I did, and you said, *'I'm going to sleep until I wake up naturally today. My head hurts from drinking last night...'* I will always do exactly as you say, you know."

Oof, it's been a long time since I've had that much to drink...

I went to check on the others, and Halkara must've fallen asleep while she was changing, because she was sleeping in her underwear, out for everyone to see.

Flatorte had fallen from her bed.

Kuku was the only one lying on her back while she slept, like a corpse. She apparently had to sleep very still so her ears wouldn't get tangled up.

I woke them all, and we had a light brunch.

During that time, Kuku had a lot to say to Flatorte. They really were like master and pupil.

"You can't cater too much to veteran fans. If you make it too comfortable for them, new fans will stop coming and your numbers will decline. Fans don't go out of their way to say why they move on. They just do."

Move on was just a fancy way of saying they quit being fans.

"You can keep going with lots of initial fans, but as they taper off, you'll eventually wind up playing in big music clubs just before you go on hiatus. You always need to plan for a comeback by constantly bringing in new fans."

"I'll keep that in mind. Now that you mention it, there are a lot of minstrel groups that go on hiatus after four or five years."

The two could probably maintain this relationship no matter where Kuku went.

Now, what would Demon King Pecora's ritual be like?

"Because we were invited to this music festival, Kuku also got the opportunity to perform. Both Miss Pecora and Miss Beelzebub are wonderful people," Laika said with joy, but I knew they weren't that pleasant.

"What is Pecora going to do to us? I'm a little excited but also nervous. More nervous than not. She hasn't come to see me in all this time. She's up to something…"

My bad feeling would be on the money, since these things always seemed to happen to me.

"It sounds like an important affair, and I'm sure she has plenty to do as the demon king."

Laika, you are too trusting. That's a good thing, though.

Well, there wasn't much point in being on alert now, so we headed for the arena.

I say *we*, but it was Fatla and Vania who took us there.

"Her Majesty has given us strict instructions to direct you to the seat with the best view."

"Oh, I heard she's been practicing a lot!"

We were placed in a carriage. *This is practically an escort…*

"What is she planning on doing…?" I asked the two, who were in the same carriage.

"In demon tradition, it is a ceremony in which the demon king makes a contract with the spirit of music."

"She is relatively free to choose how. The current demon king thinks that entertaining the spirit of music is the price to pay for the contract."

I kind of got it, but I kind of didn't...

The massive arena could apparently fit fifty thousand people. All the seats were full—this was the highlight of the affair. Citizens who couldn't get inside were gathered outside.

And we were sat in our reserved seats.

What is going to happen...?

At least she probably wasn't going to just do some ceremonial ritual and leave it at that...

Once the darkness of night finally fell—

A light flicked on, illuminating a special stage.

There came the demon king Pecora, wearing a dress that was more garish and frilly than usual.

"Demon King!" "Demon King!" "Deeeeeeeemooooooooon Kiiiiiiiiing!" "Long live the king!"

The venue erupted into cheers. I almost wanted to plug my ears!

"Hello! It's me, the demon king! Have you enjoyed the music festival?! I will be closing out the event!" Pecora called, facing the magic item that amplified her voice—a microphone, basically.

Then, she started singing.

Cover the world~ In darkness~ And everyone will become one~ ♪

These lyrics were as scary as Schifanoia's!

But her voice was sweet, like a fairy tale!

Deep chanting rippled across the arena in response to Pecora's singing.

Not only that, but all the demons who could create flame did so in the same rhythm, lighting up the venue.

"Don't tell me she's...an idol?!"

Darkness~ Darkness~ Twenty-four seven, three sixty-five~ ♪
It's dark wherever the light is not~ ♪

Pecora was dancing along with these inauspicious lyrics. She was really good at it.

I noticed Vania, who was sitting nearby, was waving something around that looked like a massive flower. She was a fan?!

I leaned over to ask Fatla, who was watching on with a blank expression.

"Uh, what is all this…?"

"Her Majesty wondered if there was a most efficient way to gather national spirit, and she came to this conclusion. Younger people typically aren't interested in these old-fashioned affairs and tend to ruin them, but apparently, even they get very involved with this."

"When you put it like that, it almost feels like a good plan."

"Additionally, a similar thing happened at the previous music festival. There were eight groups in total spanning five hours."

"That's way too long! Are they really going to bring out that many people…?"

Flatorte was looking on like a critic with a serious expression—she was even taking notes.

"I see. A performance-style idolization and yet still orthodox."

Idolization? So she really was an idol.

The performance of Demon King Pecora kept going.

You can have all the demon powers you want~ ♪
Make it a skull, make it a heart, make it both~ ♪
Sing until blood comes from your throat~ ♪
The greatest darkness is the greatest love~ ♪

The concepts in the lyrics were all uniform, but there were too many power words in there.

Pecora was dressed as an idol, and with her genuine ability to sing and dance, she was more of a real idol than I'd imagined.

Falfa was singing along with "**All the demon powers you want~ ♪**" and Shalsha was singing "**W-want~ ♪**" just a little bit behind. I guess Pecora was popular with kids, too.

"Now then, I'll be stepping out here for a moment. Up next, we have our percussionist unit, made of mining engineers from Ban Bababa Mine, Silver Only Please!"

Several people who looked like Cyclopes came out onstage and started making beats.

There were lots of people who took this opportunity to go to the bathroom, but I guess now was the time. I wasn't really interested in percussion, either, so I felt bad for them.

Afterward, plenty of demons wearing idol clothes appeared and belted out their tunes.

"This originated when the demon king wanted to lengthen her performance by making her underlings do it." Fatla just gave me a huge spoiler. "I believe she was only trying to hassle them at first, but once they gave it a shot themselves, they seemed to get really into it, and the scale of the event just grew and grew."

She looked like she was fighting a headache.

"The ones at the bottom are usually at the mercy of the ones on top, aren't they? I totally understand..."

"I hear she even has a secret intention to perform in the human kingdom and gain fans there."

The humans probably never suspected that was how the demons would be making contact...

It was an idol event at its core, but sometimes strange sideshows came into the mix.

Fighsly performed a battle with some beastly-looking creature. This was like the gladiators being made to fight against wild animals in the Roman Empire...

"This is Fighsly-style slime fist! It can make any demon stronger! Please contact Fighsly if you would like to learn! I am also accepting work!"

She sure was neck-deep in her business. She was obsessed with money, as always.

And then, I realized something. Actually, that might've just been a question of time.

"Beelzebub's not in her seat."

Vania grinned. "I wonder why~ I wonder where she went~"

Honestly, it didn't even matter if she gave me an answer at this point.

"Lady Beelzebub resisted up until the very last moment, but Her Majesty pushed too hard, so she finally gave in."

Just after Fatla finished speaking, Pecora came out on the stage again.

Yep, Pecora sounded like the most popular. She might be the demon king, but she was also a truly high-caliber performer.

"It's me, the demon king! Next, we'll have a duet! All right, you can come out now!"

Beelzebub, embarrassed, stepped out onto the stage in a gaudy idol costume.

It wasn't like her regular outfit was completely unlike something an idol would wear, but this was more like an underground idol style.

"Th-this outfit came out of the agricultural administration activation project budget... This is a legitimate expenditure..."

"Yes, it is! It passed the account auditing bureau's checks!"

The people sure were understanding.

"Miss Beelzebub, you seem embarrassed, but I don't quite understand. You want to do idol things like this. I know!"

"Th-that's not true...!" Beelzebub denied it, her face red.

"But we have record of you going all out in your service job in the past."

"Wh-why do you know that?!"

Oh, right, she worked really hard at our Witch's House Café in the past... She changed her attitude and speech, too...

"You only mind because you're in front of demons right now, but

I bet if you weren't the minister of agriculture, you wouldn't mind it, right? Right? Right?"

This is bullying… This demon king really was rotten…

"F-fine! I'll do it! Hello! Beelzebub heeere! I looove spicy food! We're gonna get this over and done with today! Can't wait to hear you cheer!"

These workers have it rough, I thought, as if this had nothing to do with me.

"Oh, no, your character will die if you do that. Speak haughtily like you always do, please."

That received a hard no from the demon king.

"I-is that so, Your Majesty?"

"And please look down on all your fans! As you were, then!"

Beelzebub took a deep breath. "Wah-ha-ha! Consider yourselves blessed to hear the beautiful voice of the great, high-ranking Beelzebub! Let the tears flow! If you yawn while I'm singing, you will be executed!"

"Very well done! Then why don't we start with our first song? 'Love Triangle, Black Magic Circle'!"

After that, the two positively shone onstage.

There was one part where they flew around and did midair acrobatics as they sang.

If I summoned someone just like you~ ♪ (Pecora)
We wouldn't have to kill each other~ ♪ (Beelzebub)
But there's more value in the original~ ♪ (Beelzebub)
So we have to kill each other~ ♪ (Pecora)

The lyrics were gory, but I was willing to ignore that.

The cheers from the crowd were even louder than they had been before.

"Get to work, Minister!" "I'll have you impeached!" "You're working harder here than you do on your agriculture work!"

There even came jeers of love (?). I guess the people liked Beelzebub, too.

But there was something that made me uneasy—the way Kuku was watching the stage with glistening eyes.

"This is an option, too…"

"Hey, Kuku? You don't need to do any of this stuff, okay? I think you're perfectly fine as you have been just using your lute, okay? I'm really, really serious!"

From the second song on, Beelzebub was clearly into it, and what Pecora said about her actually liking it wasn't entirely a joke for the act.

After warming up the audience, both Beelzebub and Pecora left.

And then, everyone who performed today would come onstage to all sing the demon national anthem or something like that to close off the event.

And indeed, all the performers slowly came together so that it began to feel like a finale.

But then, Fatla pulled my hand. Vania got up, too.

"Excuse me. Come with me, please."

I had a really bad feeling about it, but I couldn't say no.

Just as I thought, I was pulled up onto the stage for the finale.

All the demons turned to look at me, wondering what this was about.

And then Pecora raised my hand up into the air.

"An announcement, everyone! This is my elder sister, Azusa, the great Witch of the Highlands!"

The arena boiled with excitement at Pecora's introduction. Boiled over, practically.

Awww… Now all the demons know about the Witch of the Highlands…

"Elder Sister, please sing the demon national anthem with us!"

"You made me a celebrity pretty quickly…"

And so I sang a song I didn't really know the words to along with the other demons.

An announcement echoed throughout the arena: "This year's music festival has now come to an end. Please take all your trash home with you."

"There's a lot I could say, but the top of the list is that it was really fun."

"I'm very happy to hear that."

I told Fatla, who had kept her calm composure the entire time, how I felt.

"Oh man, it was insane this year. Insane, it was! Insanely insane!" Vania was muttering to herself like a video on an endless loop, so she was useless.

As state guests, we were included in the after-party.

But again, it was Fatla who had brought us there. We'd probably have to go straight to Pecora. Well, I was a performer, too, so I had the right to go to the after-party! I had been forced to perform, after all!

Pecora appeared right before me with great confidence on her face.

"How was it, Elder Sister? I worked very hard for this. I whittled down as much state business as I could in order to practice!"

I probably shouldn't tell her that was the one thing she shouldn't be whittling down on.

"Yeah, Pecora, it was impressive." I patted her head, also as a way to tell her she did good work.

She beamed happily, like a puppy, so I guess it was worth it.

"He-he-he! Thank you!"

It wouldn't hurt to have such a troublemaker little sister, I suppose.

And since I got the feeling that Beelzebub was trying to avoid me, I went to her myself.

"You're not bad at singing."

"Th-that's because you can leave anything to me and it won't be that hard..."

"You could dress up like that and perform in the human world. You'd be a hit."

"You do not have to say that! I will not do it!"

It still sounded like it was embarrassing for her. This was on a different scale from the Witch's House Café.

She'd probably end up doing it if I kept pestering her, so I'd stop it there. I felt bad for her.

"Look, I'm complimenting you. Aren't you happy about that?" Today I was going to be a little more aggressive.

Beelzebub didn't seem totally out of it, either. "Th-thank...you," she said, her face red, and turned to the side.

She wasn't very straightforward, and that did check the box for cuteness, in its own way.

But when my daughters came up to her with, "It was really good!" and "That was a great performance," she suddenly got all excited.

"That is my true skill!" she cried. She really changed her attitude depending on who she was talking to...

And there was one other significant matter that needed addressing.

Kuku came up to me, looking like she had a very important announcement to make.

"Miss Azusa, since I've received quite the volume of work requests here in the castle town, I've decided to stay. I will work here for three weeks before returning to the royal capital."

"Yeah, that's a good idea. But promise me one thing."

I placed my hands on hers. For the first time, I realized how small Kuku was.

Her long ears made it feel like she was taller than me, but she really wasn't.

"If you ever feel like you can't take it anymore, or you think you can't do it anymore, then come back to the house in the highlands. Your worries won't solve themselves if you fret about them alone. Come by anytime. You're our family, so you can come whenever you like."

"O-okay..." Kuku's voice was quavering behind tears.

Oh dear, I've made her cry again. I wasn't happy about that.

"And be sure to eat. Take care not to end up fainting again. Oh, I made you promise two things..."

This time, Kuku smiled and said, "Of course!"

It might be nice to do another going-away party for her back at the house, but it would probably be best to just say our good-byes here.

Well, there was no problem at all! All the strange people I'd met were happily doing their thing all over the world, and we did come into contact occasionally.

That was when Fatla and Vania came over in a rush.

"Oh, what happened?"

"Pardon me, but you've received several requests from several theaters to perform... The first one is called *Talk Show: As the Demon Lord's Big Sister*. Most of them are roughly the same..."

Ugh! My stage appearance is affecting me already?!

"There are lots of interview requests from newspapers as well! You're so popular!"

"No, Vania, that doesn't make me happy! I don't want to be popular!"

It sounded like my notability was skyrocketing here in the demon lands... *I wonder if I'll start being treated like a demon boss, and people from the human lands will start coming to defeat me...*

I'll just pray that my little house in the highlands never gets called a horrible, scary dungeon...

That day, I went all the way to the southern part of the country to pick herbs.

"Madam Teacher, what turn of events brought you out here?" asked my apprentice, Halkara, who was there with me. I sometimes forgot, but Halkara was still an apprentice of mine. She was saying it herself, so there was no mistaking it.

"I remembered what the purpose of being a witch was and decided to do something witchlike. Lately, I feel like we've been dealing with unemployed undead, starving minstrels, and the like—all things that have nothing to do with my real job..."

Pondeli the undead was currently running a card game shop in the demon castle town. Kuku the almiraj had also recently undergone a change of character and was gaining tons of real experience as a singer.

I was glad both of them were turning out well. But neither of those things had anything to do with my witchy work.

I was the Witch of the Highlands, after all.

"I completely understand. I have to create new products that can beat out that Witch of the Grotto."

"It must be rough having a rival now..."

After Eno, the Witch of the Grotto, made a hit out of her Mandragora pills, she released a product called Forest Elixir. It was a concentrated drink meant to be diluted in water for daily use, so now Halkara had competition for Halkara Pharmaceuticals.

"Now, I will just have to find an herb that contains incredibly healthy ingredients to widen the lead! I must venture farther afield for my herb-gathering!"

Let's do this! said Halkara's expression as she struck a fighting pose.

Her motives didn't seem totally and wholly pure, but it wasn't really a bad thing.

By the way, Laika was following behind us, and for some reason she was riding on an elephant.

No, really, she was riding on an elephant.

Laika didn't have any knowledge of plants, so she'd looked bored out of her mind until she discovered and befriended an elephant as we were walking around the forest. It let her ride on its back.

"It's just as fun as a horse but in a different way!"

"Bareeee! Bowa-bowa-bo!"

Baree etc. were the sounds the elephant made. Its cry was strange, like the air itself was splitting.

There were apparently monsters lurking around this forest, but with an elephant following behind us, they were all getting scared and running away. We didn't spot a single one. It was the elephant's seal of safety.

I would be fine with whatever came at us, but it was still considerably dangerous for Halkara.

Our search for herbs wasn't going so well, though. Especially for Halkara.

"Eeeek! The spiders are so big! This stinkbug is so stinky!"

It even felt like we were carefully setting off each and every one of the forest's natural traps.

It was at times like these that Halkara never defied my expectations.

"This is strange... I'm the one leading us along this path with Halkara behind me, but she's the one always getting hurt... Maybe she should be leading the way through the forest instead..."

"Ah! There's a dangerous snake! Please stay away!"

Maybe we should put a rain check on our herb search... Halkara was going to get hurt sooner or later.

"Why do these snakes keep going after me?! And if I run away, more of them come! Why are there three of them now?!"

Are you wearing perfume that attracts snakes...? You're just a magnet for trouble.

Halkara changed her course across the forest, so I gave chase. There was the risk of losing her if I didn't keep my eyes on her.

Then suddenly, everything opened up before us.

There was a magnificent pastoral view.

Plants that looked like rice were growing from pools of water.

It was like home in Japan. I mean, my hometown wasn't a farming village, so I didn't have any experience with fields, but it felt nostalgic.

"Wow! It's a rice-growing region."

Laika followed us on her elephant.

"The southern part of the kingdom cultivates something called rice. Other regions depend largely on bread, but they also eat rice here."

"Man, this brings me back. I lived in a rice-eating culture in my previous life."

And Halkara, by the way, appeared to be a big hit with the snakes as they wrapped around her arms and legs. They didn't seem like they were going to bite her.

"Awww, they're cuter than I thought. What lovely round eyes they have!"

She sure sounded calm. I guess I wouldn't have to cast any Cure Poison spells.

"Oh yeah, would there be any shop around here where we could eat some rice?"

"I believe so. But what should we do about our herb hunting?"

"We'll put it on hold."

We entered the nearby town and went into a restaurant. Our seats were at a table outside beneath an awning, probably because it was so humid. It felt nice and open.

What came to us was a dish of red beans and rice with spicy chicken sitting on top. I forgot what it was called. The language in the south was somewhat different, so I didn't understand it very well.

"Okay then, I'm digging in!" Like the ex-Japanese person I was, I pressed my hands together and started to eat.

I took my first bite and noticed a slightly different texture from what I would call a normal bowl of rice.

The combination was so gummy. No, that wasn't the right word—maybe doughy. It was like red bean rice but even softer. And the rice itself was more like red rice, too.

It wasn't that the rice was cooked wrong—that was just the kind of rice it was. In Japanese terms, this would be like sticky rice.

Laika and Halkara didn't seem to take to it very well. They were eating their dish with a strange look on their faces.

"This dish oddly sticks to your stomach, doesn't it?"

"I believe I prefer bread. It does feel like this will fill you up, though."

It must've been because of the spices, but it leaned more toward what I'd call "ethnic," so you'd either love it or hate it. It tasted like something for especially sensitive eaters.

I always thought the girls spending nine hundred yen for lunch were being extravagant, but I was going to die from overwork anyway, so maybe I should've splurged a bit more on lunch.

Beans and sticky rice, huh? And there was wheat, too.

An idea suddenly came to me.

I could make some Japanese sweets, couldn't I?

We had beans, so I could make something like sweet bean paste, and I bet I could make the wrappings of *manju* buns out of flour. Next was the mochi. I should be able to make that out of this sticky rice.

And my motive for making sweets would be to see the smiles on Falfa's and Shalsha's faces. The end.

Laika was better at cooking than I was, and Halkara wasn't too bad at it (even though some weird things ended up in the mix). I hadn't heard it enough: "Mommy, you're a good cook!"

They still complimented me, but it was more out of gratitude for the person who made their food, not the sort of reaction you'd hear if something was *truly* delicious.

So if I made a ton of *manju*, my daughters might acknowledge me as a mother who was good at making sweets.

Not bad, not bad at all.

But it was possible *manju* already existed in this world. If I boldly declared it was my original creation and it turned out someone had thought of it first, that would be pretty embarrassing. So I should investigate.

"Hey, Laika, Halkara, do you know what kinds of sweets they have in this region?"

Laika tilted her head, but Halkara answered, "Crunchies." It was a rather silly name. "It's because they make a crunchy noise when you bite into them, so they call them crunchies. It sounds like something a child would call them, doesn't it?"

"Huh. I'd want to try that."

"It might be on the menu here. They serve the classics."

Then I'll order it right now. I asked the waiter for it.

What we got was very thin and round.

It was like a *takoyaki senbei* but even flatter and wider. I took a bite, and it was sweet. And crunchy.

"Wow. It has a simple taste, but it's better than I thought."

"It would be lovely with a beer."

"Halkara, you sure have a thing for alcohol despite how you pass out almost right away."

As Halkara and I chatted, Laika ate silently.

I completely understood, since it was the texture of a light snack. It made you want to just eat them all.

But it wasn't the kind of sweet I was imagining.

Afterward, I asked the restaurant staff if there were any steamed sweets in the region, but nothing immediately came to their minds. I was probably in the clear. *Manju* shouldn't be a thing here!

Wait, I thought it was in the Muromachi period or so in Japan that the *mantou* came from China, and since it first came to a Zen temple—they couldn't eat the meat, so they settled on filling the wrapper with something sweet.

Nowadays, *manju* and sweet bean *Anman* and meaty *Nikuman* all looked different, but their ancestors were practically the same thing.

And while I was at it, if you squinted at *Anpan*, you could call it a relative of the *manju*. They both had an outer shell made of flour and a filling inside.

On the other hand, the mochi line of sweets all used sticky rice. Something along those lines might already exist, but there wasn't any copyright on this stuff, so I could sell a bunch. If I didn't call them an original, then there would be no problem.

"You two go find a shop that sells beans later."

"Oh, there are plenty of beans that are good for one's health, aren't there?!"

Sorry, Halkara, I think my motives might be impure this time around.

Afterward, I searched for red sweet beans that were as close to sweet *adzuki* beans as I could find. Then, I purchased a large amount of sticky rice while I was at it.

The other two seemed to think we were going to re-create these southern dishes at home, but they were wrong.

When I got home, I went straight to trying to re-create the sweet bean paste and *manju* shell through trial and error.

I wasn't an artisan or anything in my past life, so I would just have to learn through failure.

I didn't have any work, luckily, so I had plenty of time.

"Madam Teacher is trying to make something. She looks so serious!" is what Halkara said, saddling me with meaningless guilt, but there were no problems besides that.

Additionally, I had Flatorte eat all my failed attempts when she was hungry and just wanted to munch on something.

"I believe they're getting tastier, Mistress."

"That's a relief. I'll bring you some if I manage to complete it."

Making the *anko* went comparatively quicker. I sweetened it with sugar and honey and such, boiled the beans, and made something close enough. Man, sweeteners were the best.

But the shell was proving troublesome. It wasn't really getting very big with just flour.

Would I need to use baking soda? In short, I probably would. I wanted some if it existed, but I didn't really know where they'd sell it.

Or would I have to leaven it with malted rice? I didn't even know where to look for malt.

It might work if I put yams in... I'd seen *manju* that had yams in it before. But I wasn't really sure where yams grew around here.

Eventually, I ended up making a few gluey shells, and since they were basically edible, I brought them all to Flatorte.

"I think they need to be a little moister."

"I know. I'll think of something and bring 'em over."

And then, just as I was getting sick of all my trial and error—

I found the perfect mixture!

I wasn't going to share my trade secret.

It was witchlike to have secrets, so it was fine.

"I took a bite, and it is exactly like a *manju*! He-he-he, he-he-he-he! I did it; I did it! This is the work of a lifetime!"

I was at peak excitement!

"That's fantastic, Mistress! You succeeded on your hundred and eighteenth try!"

"Thank you, too, Flatorte! And you just told me how many times I failed, didn't you…?"

Rosalie appeared afterward and corrected her, since I'd failed five times before Flatorte started watching, so it was *really* a hundred and twenty-three times. Just as things changed after three hundred years killing slimes, perfection would come if I just kept at making *manju*.

Now then, it was time to have Falfa and Shalsha take a taste—or so I was tempted to do, but I should first give some to Flatorte, who had watched me this whole time.

"Here you go. It's right out of the pot, so it's a little hot."

"I have a sensitive tongue, so I'll be careful. I'm okay with cold food, though."

She did breathe ice, after all.

Flatorte's eyes widened in surprise. Her tail started twitching.

"Oh! This is delicious! This is new, something I've never had before!"

All right! Next, my daughters!

Falfa and Shalsha had been in their room reading books this entire time.

Falfa was reading *Arithmetic and Logic*, and Shalsha was reading *What Is Time?*

This was always the case, but they were abnormally difficult books. I didn't understand them at all. I thought if they took the right steps, they could become professors with those minds.

"Hey, how about snack time? Don't you get sleepy using your brain so much?"

"But we finished with dinner already. It's not snack time."

"It's been a while since we finished eating, too, so it's not really dessert, either."

They calmly passed judgment on me.

"A-anyway, Mommy made a yummy sweet snack for you to eat!"

They were round and of a brownish color—just like *manju* should be. I presented them a plate with a few sitting on it.

"Don't you want something sweet after using your brain? You can make even more progress if you have some! Eat, eat!"

I might've been a little too pushy, but they each reached out to take one.

First, Falfa popped it into her mouth.

And immediately, her expression brightened! My victory was certain!

"It's so yummy! It's really yummy! You're incredible, Mommy! I've never had anything like this before! You're so good at making sweets, Mommy!"

"Thank you. I've been wanting to hear that for ages!"

I savored the joy.

Next was Shalsha. Their tastes were very similar, so I wasn't that worried anymore.

"Mm... How exquisite..."

Her eyes were closed, and she was shivering slightly. She then reached out to take a second one. Her expression hadn't changed much, but she wouldn't have responded like that if she didn't like it.

"Mom, what's this called?" Shalsha was the type who always wanted to know where things came from. This time was no different.

"It's called *manju*."

"*Manjoo*... I think there's a place with the same name in the west," Shalsha said, going to retrieve a geographical dictionary from her bookshelf. I didn't think *manju* would be in there... *It's not a place name anyway.*

"There it is: Manjoo. Earl Lugness of Manjoo is famous. There's no account here of these sweets."

"That's because they're unrelated... A total coincidence."

But I didn't really like the idea that people would think this was an original of the Manjoo region. I was the one who created it here in this world.

And on the flip side, if *manju* ended up getting popular and spreading, it was possible that the people of Manjoo would be perplexed as to why it was named after their land.

Shalsha flipped through the dictionary as Falfa munched on the treat. It probably wasn't the healthiest thing to eat after dinner, but I'd allow it for today.

"They're yummy, but it'd be better if they were cuter!"

And she asked for cuteness. Wait, did *manju* need to be cute?!

"See, Mommy, it doesn't have a face or anything on it. Wouldn't it be more adorable if it had a face?"

"That's a new one... Wait, some *manju* were printed with companies' names on them, so I guess not..."

That being said, it'd be creepy if we put a lifelike face on it, so we had to deal with that. Maybe an animal face? But what was an animal with an easy-to-recognize face?

"They're sort of shaped like slimes," Shalsha murmured, popping a whole one into her mouth. "*O hourse, haim ahnt hweet hou.*"

I think she was saying, *Of course, slimes aren't sweet, though.*

What she said suddenly gave me inspiration.

I could make a slime face easily. It was super simple. I just had to heat something up and press it against them.

"Got it. Wait a sec!"

I had Flame magic to heat things up, so I just did that to the first metal object I found and pressed it against the *manju* to make the eyes.

"Okay, they look more like slimes now!"

And then, my daughters' faces started to glow.

The *manju* sure were cute with slime faces. Children would probably like them, too.

"Slimes are yummy!"

"Slimes are delicious."

Watching the two slime girls eat them looked a little like cannibalism, but they shared nothing in common with real slimes besides the shape, so it was fine.

And I got another Halkara-like spark of brilliance.

I could sell these.

I didn't want to go as far as making a business out of them and

getting rich, but if I brought them to Flatta, the people there would probably be happy for it.

As for the name, *manju* would only remind people of the place Manjoo, so I guess we'd go with "edible slimes."

I used everyone I knew as my test group.

First up were my family members Laika and Halkara.

"It's so soft, Lady Azusa!"

"This would be a great product!"

Their reactions were just as I expected, thank you. I would keep those comments in mind.

Next, figuring she probably didn't have any work at this hour, I summoned Beelzebub using magic.

However, it seemed like she was doing overtime, since she appeared with a quill in hand. *Oops...she'll probably complain again...*

"This is, like, another unbelievable situation, is it not? It's not because you got your hands on a nice bottle of booze, yes? I do not mind either way. Speak up."

That introductory remark made it hard to say. *But I'm gonna say it. She said it was okay, so I'm gonna say it.*

"I made sweets we're calling 'edible slimes,' so have a taste. They're a big hit right now!"

As I thought, Beelzebub still didn't seem to buy it (which meant we were even after Beelzebub came and pushed things on me out of the blue), but she popped one into her mouth anyway.

"Mm! I believe you're on the right track!"

"Right?! I did pretty well, don't you think?"

"You might even be more suited to making these things than any medicine!"

"That's a rude thing to say to a witch! You better take that back!"

The test group round seemed to be a success for the moment.

"All right, we'll test it tomorrow and sell them in Flatta!" I said, and my daughters heard me.

"I wanna play shop!"

"There are things to be gained from honest work."

We weren't *playing* shop, but we had only one thing to sell, and the two of them could even do it on their own.

All right, I'll let them help me!

Early the next morning.

My two daughters and I went to the mayor's house and said we wanted to open up a shop.

"Excuse me. We made some sweets, so we would like to sell them if you have an open spot."

"Set up a table in the market and sell them there. It's sunny today, so you shouldn't need an awning."

It was decided right away.

I was thankful for the trust and good track record I'd built up over these three hundred years. We borrowed a table from the community center and made a simple setup.

And the reason we came so early was because it would take a while to get everything ready. The villagers were most active in the morning, so if we took our time, we'd miss the prime shopping hours.

And of course, we had what we needed.

"Shalsha, bring it out."

"Understood."

Shalsha spread out a sign advertising EDIBLE SLIMES.

There was an illustration of the delicious-looking merchandise on display in crates and an enlarged picture of one of them on top.

And then it said, MAGNIFICENT FLAVOR, REVITALIZING AND NOURISHING—CAREFULLY PRODUCED BY THE WITCH OF THE HIGHLANDS: EDIBLE SLIMES.

The expressions were a little stiff, but, well, this was for fun. And they had nutrients in them because they were food, so the line about being nourishing wasn't a lie.

Shalsha was good at drawing, so I'd asked her to draw the picture.

"Yaaay, it's a shop; it's a shop! Gross profiiits! ♪ Break-even pooo-ints! ♪ Sunk cooosts! ♪"

Falfa was fidgeting in excitement, but her choice of words was a little too vivid. Was it because she had been reading math books...?

Behind our price tags, we lined up the merchandise: one for seventy gold; a four pack for two hundred and fifty gold; an eight pack for five hundred gold; a sixteen pack for a thousand gold; a thirty-two pack for two thousand gold.

I thought the thirty-two pack was a lovely sight. It was like a gift box.

"All right! Let's sell!" I mentally rolled up my sleeves.

"Mommy, Mommy! Why don't we cut one into four quarters and place them on the side for people to try? No one's seen this food before, so we should have them try it first."

"I see, Falfa! That's clever."

"And maybe we should write down where we sourced our beans and wheat from! There might be some customers who want to know."

"...You're a little too serious about this, aren't you, Falfa?"

It almost felt like I'd brought Halkara along. Was this what playing shop was like? Did kids these days get serious about playing house? Was guidance about how to deal with litigious customers part of the norm now?

Come to think of it, they always did get pretty into it when they played house...

We hadn't set any hours, so our opening time was when the villagers started coming out to shop.

Before I could even psyche myself up for it, the villagers immediately gathered in an endless stream.

"The great Witch of the Highlands has made something new." "Oooh, it's shaped like a slime." "It's sooo cuuute!"

Falfa held the plate of sample edible slimes and presented them to the customers. She was sharp when it came to this stuff...

"Everyone, please have a taste! If you like it, please buy!"

The crowd of villagers popped pieces of the edible slimes into their mouths, one after the other.

These people had never had the sweet bean paste called *anko* before, so I wondered if they would be okay, but there was no need to worry at all. I could tell this was a win just by looking at their faces.

"This black cream inside the fluffy bread is so good!" "What a tender sweet!" "My mouth is so happy right now!" "The great Witch of the Highlands really *is* amazing!"

The nonfans of the *manju* were few and far between, from what I could tell.

The villagers were captivated.

"I'll take that big box there!" "One eight pack, please!" "Same, but two of 'em!"

They flew off the table. *Yes, yes! This is the thrill of commerce!*

And Falfa, by the way, was unusually courteous in dealing with our customers.

"Thank you very much! They will taste much better if you warm them up a little! Come back again!"

Why is she so good at dealing with customers?

"Big Sister does not cut corners when we play. When she was pretending to be a cricket, she wanted to observe how it jumped and what it ate," Shalsha, who was still a little nervous, explained.

"I guess I started it..."

"There's no doubt that since she's playing with real money and real customers, she's being especially serious."

This wasn't a game, though. It was just pure customer service.

I would've been expecting something a little fancier if I was playing shop. We could've created the ambiance of an old, long-standing Japanese sweets shop...

Either way, the edible slimes were super popular, and I was thankful for that. Times like these, we usually sold so much more than what was believable for the population of the village, and it looked like it was going to be the same thing again.

And then an unexpected customer appeared.

"You've been working hard, Madam Teacher."

Halkara had come to the front of the line. It looked like she'd waited her turn.

"Don't tell me you came to express your appreciation?"

"I was watching your sales from a little ways away. I believe you'll be able to sell in other regions like this. Please let me sell them in Nascúte. I can guarantee employees as well!"

She came to turn this into a business…

"If you're here for negotiations, please come this way!"

And Falfa was really into it…

After discussions with Halkara, we came to the following conclusions:

- Halkara would use her employees to sell in the villages of Flatta and Nascúte (but mainly Nascúte).
- The product would be called Flatta Cakes and would act as an advertisement for the village of Flatta.
- They would first be made when the family had free time, but in the instance that their popularity exploded, the recipe would be taught to employees of Halkara Pharmaceuticals.

I hadn't really been planning on making a profitable business out of it, but it was probably fine to sell them in nearby places like Nascúte.

While the edible slimes were a huge hit, I started brainstorming my next product.

That would be mochi made with sticky rice. Well, there were many kinds of sweets that had mochi in them. If it was too sticky, then it came with the risk of getting stuck in someone's throat, so I decided to make oak-leaf-wrapped mochi.

Flatorte devoured all my test runs this time, too, like staff eating leftovers. This was one of those times when it was great to have a hungry dragon around.

Compared to when I was making *manju*, I finished this one fairly quickly.

I added the slime eye marks this time, too.

And because I could, I placed the mochi on top of a leaf and called it finished.

"I call it: leaf slime!"

Flatorte was the first person to taste test.

"Mm, it feels weighty in my stomach. This could be good for breakfast. The bean paste inside isn't so bad, either."

"It is rice. So it's probably heavy."

"First, let me eat fifteen of them for now."

Fifteen was a little much to start with *for now*.

Then, I had my daughters try them.

"It's yummy! I love you, Mommy!" "You're good at cooking, Mom."

I wanted Shalsha to say *I love you, Mommy!* with that much enthusiasm one day, but her whole personality would have to change for that to happen, so I didn't mind so much.

Of course, I knew very well that Shalsha loved her mommy. Very, very well. Better than Beelzebub, at least, and that was what really mattered.

"Mom, I'd enjoy this with some tea."

Shalsha was the one who came up with the idea, so I poured her a cup.

I made it a little strong so that it would pair well with the leaf slime.

Shalsha took a bite of her treat and sipped her tea.

"Hoooo, mmmm. This is refreshing."

Then, her eyelids immediately slipped downward, and a gentle smile crossed her face.

Shalsha's precious smile! Yes, what a great thing to see!

I was suddenly seized by the impulse to hug her then and there, but I resisted. Her mother I may be, but it was still suspicious behavior. Such patience was necessary.

"If only I had a cat on my lap. That would be the best."

I imagined her as an old grandma taking a rest on a porch outside.

Cats are cute, so I get it.

"Your candy goes well with tea, Mommy! Yeah, I understand what Shalsha's saying!"

As always, Falfa was completely agreeing with her.

I'd even become a witch to preserve that smile (well, I was already a witch).

Okay then, I'd have to get selling these leaf slimes. I had to tell Halkara.

I appreciated Halkara's offer to provide guaranteed employees. Selling something was a long-term commitment. Making these was just an extension of a hobby, so I couldn't wake up every day at the same time to prepare for it.

The company system would cover all those problems for me.

The company would make up for my limitations as an individual and play a role in expansion. Companies did have their good points, of course, and I would make use of them.

I had Halkara taste a leaf slime (whose name was practically the same as leaf mochi), and she gave a big seal of approval.

"Yes, we will absolutely sell this, too! This and edible slimes will be our two main attractions. This will cover all our bases!"

"If you say they'll be a hit, Halkara, then there's no room for doubt."

The next day, I got to watch them being sold in the town of Nascúte.

New Product: Leaf Slimes! Just In! A New Flavor! The Witch of the Highlands's True Skill!

The words danced across the sign behind an employee getting ready to open shop.

"I feel embarrassed looking on from over here…"

"There's nothing to be embarrassed about! Stand up proud!"

And then, it was opening time. The employee raised her voice: "We are now open for business! We have a new product! Come try it!" And the people came in droves.

The population here was higher than Flatta's, not to mention all the visiting out-of-towners, so the area right in front of the shop was bustling.

"Ohhh, this is exhilarating… It is nice to see people buy what you've made…"

"Isn't it? They'll probably sell out before noon. Producing them en masse will bring us more money, but we would be getting our priorities backward if the taste went down in quality, so I believe we should continue as is."

What pleased me most of all were the smiles on the faces of the customers who bought them.

At first, I just wanted to make my daughters happy, but now that I was bringing smiles to more people, there was nothing better.

I could hear people saying, "Wow, the great Witch of the Highlands is incredible." *That's it—praise me more.*

"The great Witch really is good with food and drink, isn't she?" "The Witch's House Café was great, too."

Hmm…? Something about my reputation isn't quite right…

"I guess this is the great Witch's forte." "She probably realized she's more suited to this than medicine." "It's nice to discover your strengths."

At that moment, I realized I'd made a mistake.

The reason I'd gone south in the first place was to make medicine, but now I was getting attention for my sweets. The medicine-making part of me was stepping back!

The employee was yelling, "We have a new product from the great Witch of the Pastries!"

Please don't give me a nickname like that! I'm still the Witch of the Highlands!

"This is a wonderful new creation, from three hundred years of wisdom living in the highlands to make excellent sweets!"

I didn't start living there to make desserts!

"A three-hundred-year-old tradition lives on in these sweets! The epitome of old meets new!"

Please don't make this sound like my shop's been around since the medieval era!

Maybe I should just give up on making a name for myself in medicine...

But that wouldn't make me a witch anymore, would it...?

I nibbled on a leaf slime as I pondered my identity.

It was perfect—lightly sweet.

This could take over the world.

—Wait, I can't forget about my slow life...

FATLA AND VANIA

AW, I WANT TO USE MY BOSS'S MONEY TO GO TO THE BATHS...

I'M SORRY. MY LITTLE SISTER IS A HANDFUL...

Leviathan sisters who work as Beelzebub's secretaries. They can transform into giant dragons, and they transport Azusa and company to the demon lands as well as look after them. The elder sister, Fatla, is a stable and capable girl. The younger sister, Vania, is ditzy but a good cook.

ENO

The immortal Witch of the Grotto, who reveres Azusa as her senior. Though she has superior potion-making skills, her unwillingness to let others see her efforts prevented her from making progress. After Azusa reasoned with her, she changed her ways. She's actively working now, but she sometimes butts heads with her industry competitor Halkara.

AS LONG AS I'M ALIVE, I WANT TO WIN.

NO! I WON'T WORK!

PONDELI

An undead catperson. Hates working. Loves games. A tried-and-true shut-in, she stayed in her room until she died and then stayed there even after death. Beelzebub picked her up, and she now runs a game lounge in demon country.

A little while had passed since I started being called the Witch of the Pastries.

I was in Flatta shopping with my daughters.

It was all a familiar sight. More people were wearing heavy coats because of the chill, but in a way, you could say that was the only difference.

On the way home, I dropped by the guild to exchange for money the magic stones from the slimes I'd killed.

Our village guild didn't have many workers. Natalie was sitting there prim and proper.

"Hello, here's this batch of magic stones."

I produced the bag stuffed with the stones.

"All right, then, I'll start counting them. There's sixty in here. That comes out to twelve thousand gold."

That was about twelve thousand yen. Even though I was taking my time saving up my money, it was perfect, since I could kill slimes in my free time.

Laika was killing much more on her own, so she exchanged her own money separately. She probably felt so accomplished whenever she saw how many magic stones she'd collected.

"Great Witch, don't you think that you could make much more

money if you just concentrated on making desserts? If you do, I think Miss Halkara might be making quite a profit at her factory there."

Natalie was starting to become aware of the Witch of the Pastries...

"Killing slimes is a regular habit for me. Even if I had millions of gold, I'd still want to get that thousand, you know? I'm not exactly sad to get it."

"That's true, I suppose. If you want it, you want it."

People weren't generally upset to receive money, and the more there was, the happier they were.

"Oh, right, right. A letter came for you, great Witch."

Falfa gingerly accepted the letter Natalie held out for us.

"A letter, huh? From whom, I wonder? I hope it's not a request to go kill some weird monsters."

Now, let me explain how the mail system in this world worked.

And let me start by amending what I just said: There was no public mail "system." There were public offices that sent notifications to child organizations, but that was different. We're talking about Ordinary Person A sending something to Ordinary Person B.

The way they did this was that if there was someone headed in the direction of where Person B lived, Person A handed the letter over to them. If the carrier wasn't going all the way to the letter's destination, then they handed the letter off to someone else. The letter was like a hitchhiker.

And that was how this letter eventually came to the village of Flatta.

I think Japan in the Middle Ages had a similar mail "system." It was common for people to receive letters almost half a year since they were written. I could imagine a love letter being written then arriving at its destination after the writer was already in a different relationship.

Additionally, when the demons brought over invitations, they had someone specifically for that. In the human world, too, when it was urgent that Person B get something quickly, someone would take on that role.

Needless to say, that was really expensive.

It was almost like sending out a messenger.

So what could this be?

One of the advantages of this crude system was that something unspecific like "The great Witch who might live in the town of Flatta" would eventually find its way to me. As long as it made it here, someone would keep it in a place my family frequented.

Falfa opened the envelope and started reading the letter inside. She shouldn't have done that if it was for Halkara or Laika, but if it was addressed vaguely to my house, then it was fine.

"Hmm, Falfa didn't know this was a thing."

Falfa's comment didn't tell me much.

She handed the letter to Shalsha to read over when she was finished, but it was still hard to tell, since Shalsha was reading silently.

Still, judging by their reactions, it didn't seem like unhappy news or something that would disappoint them.

"Hey, you two, who is it from?"

"It's from something called the World Spirit Summit!"

"World Spirit Summit?"

I'd never heard of that before. *Summit* implied it was some kind of conference.

But I couldn't say it was totally irrelevant. My daughters were slime spirits, after all.

"Do you know about this summit?"

Falfa said, "Nuh-uh," and Shalsha shook her head.

Then it was very possible that no one else in the house would know about it.

"Mom, to summarize what it says, spirits occasionally get together to hold the World Spirit Summit, and both Shalsha and Falfa have been invited."

"Huh... But you're not registered with them or anything, so I'm impressed they knew you're slime spirits..."

"The invitation says they heard about us from a rumor on the wind."

This world really was sloppy.

"We should be able to make it. It's close by, too. They're apparently gathering at night by Lake Nanterre."

"That is close."

The name of this province, Nanterre, came from the beautiful Lake Nanterre in these equally beautiful highlands.

It was close enough to be in the same province, but it was a little too far for a day's walk, so I'd never gone. I hadn't been doing much sightseeing these past three hundred years.

"We did get invited, so Falfa wants to go!"

"Shalsha is also interested."

"Of course. I'm wondering what it's all about, and I'm not even a spirit. And I bet it'll be full of spirits, right? I don't remember ever seeing a fire spirit or a water spirit, so I'm not totally sure if they even exist."

They had to—this was a fantasy world, after all—but I hadn't done any fantasy staple activities like dungeon diving. I guess I wouldn't have met any.

"Do you want to go, too, Mommy? You should come with us!"

Falfa was pointing to a spot on the letter.

It said, "Parent or guardian accompaniment allowed."

I see. Maybe the wind also said they were child spirits.

"Of course. It would be dangerous to let you two just go by yourselves, especially if this is a kidnapping pretending to be a summit. I should go along."

"Yaaay! A trip with Mommy!" Falfa hugged me. She shouldn't get so worked up inside the guild, but I was happy that she was hugging me. She could hug me as much as she wanted.

Shalsha wasn't as forward as Falfa, but she looked so sad that I decided to give her a big hug on the way home. My style was to treat both sisters equally.

Natalie was a little shocked. "That was quick for such a terrifying summit. Well, you are the great Witch, after all..."

"Is the general opinion that spirits are not easy to deal with?"

"It's a legend, but they say that many spirits are capricious. You also hear about some who don't have the same values as humans. For example, a lightning spirit may want to strike a human with lightning just to test it out, and the human ends up dying..."

Maybe like children catching and dissecting insects.

Falfa and Shalsha didn't do cruel things like that, though.

I called it *cruel*, but the concept was one of the values for adult humans, too. Sometimes people did similar things without really thinking. Nobody thought it was cruel to cut vegetables to use for soup.

"In that case, I really should go. Spirits would probably be peaceful on their own, though. And it was in some way calling itself a summit, so I guess it shouldn't be too dangerous."

And so I decided to attend the World Spirit Summit.

Laika offered to escort us to Lake Nanterre, but I wanted to take the opportunity to have a nice relaxing time with my girls. And that's just what we did.

We first walked to Nascúte, and from there we took a cart.

A slow journey wasn't so bad once in a while. Laika's ability to change into a dragon and carry us was very convenient, but we couldn't get too accustomed to it. It was good to enjoy the road to the destination, too.

"He-he-he! Traveling! Traveling! Traveling with Mommy! Wheeee!"

Falfa was so excited about it. It was like a field trip for them.

"Your bag is stuffed full, isn't it? Did you really need to bring all that?"

I also read the World Spirit Summit invitation, but it didn't say to bring anything. The most we needed was probably just stuff to write with.

"Yeah! There was a lot I wanted to prepare!"

"I see. I'm excited to attend, as well."

Incidentally, Shalsha sat on the other side of me, and she looked so sleepy the entire time. Actually, I think she *was* asleep.

There were lots of people who dozed off on trains, apparently because the rhythm of the train rocked you right to sleep. Maybe this cart was doing something similar.

"Shalsha was so excited yesterday, she couldn't sleep."

"That sounds just like someone before a field trip!"

That took me back… The day before any field trip in elementary school, I could never fall asleep, so I think I put music on to help me. It'd put me to sleep before I knew it.

Shalsha ended up falling asleep hugging her bag. She was leaning right up against me.

"Shalsha's asleep," Falfa commented, and soon she did the same and was leaning against me.

"Awww, you cute kids."

It was fair to say my motherly joy had never been higher.

Personally, I was so happy with our trip that I could probably end it now and still be more than satisfied, but our main event was the World Spirit Summit.

What was this summit going to be like?

Along the way, we stayed the night at a town halfway there, then the second evening, we finally arrived at Lake Nanterre.

This was a tourist destination, and the scenery before us was stunning.

The most appropriate thing for such a sight was to not say anything at all, but if I had to say something, it would be about how deep the blue of the lake was. It was almost an ultramarine, a perfect match for the green of the highlands.

It was as though someone had placed a gigantic mirror in a high-elevation spot.

"Woooow! It's so prettyyy! And so biiig!"

"Writers and artists have praised this view since ancient times..."

Both of them were expressing their impressions in their own way.

But—

"This is where we're supposed to meet, right? No one's here."

That was right—I didn't see any people around the lake. Well, they were spirits, so not strictly "people."

"The sun should be setting soon. Even if there were any tourists, they would all be at the inns back at the foot of the mountain by now."

"It's just like Falfa says. It'd be weird to see anyone here at this time."

"According to the invitation, it says we should be at the part of the lake that juts out a bit. I think that's up ahead."

We all headed to the spot Shalsha pointed out. Still nobody.

"Were we tricked? Is this a joke? But this isn't a very impressive way to trick us..."

"Mom, the invitation says we're all gathering at night. It's too early to say it's nighttime. This probably means we should wait a little more."

"You're right. We'll relax here, then. It might be nice to watch the sunset."

And as we lazed about for an hour—

I suddenly felt a number of presences.

And I mean a big number—like we'd been suddenly thrown into the middle of the marketplace in the royal capital!

And it wasn't just a feeling. People—no, spirits—were gathering in swarms.

Generally, the majority looked like humans.

Most of the women wore loose, fairly revealing dresses. Like something you'd wear at a ball. Others wore dresses with open backs, pretty close to how I imagined spirits in my head.

A great percentage of the male spirits were shirtless and had bulging muscles. That was also pretty close to what I'd made up in my head. I was thinking of those spirits who came out of lamps when you rubbed them.

I wondered if they were shirtless because they wanted to show off their muscles, or if they wanted to show off their muscles because they were shirtless.

Compared to humans, their hair was very colorful. It was just a guess, but maybe the blue-haired spirits were related to water, and the red-haired spirits were related to fire.

And some didn't take human form at all.

There were creatures who were like shaggily cut rosebushes with eyeballs and even fancy ones reminiscent of mascot characters from a magical girl comic.

I had no idea what kind of spirit they'd be. My own Falfa and Shalsha were pretty irregular themselves—it was hard to tell they were slime spirits just by looking.

And these spirits were all chatting noisily and happily.

When did they all get here?

"Woooow! There's so many!"

"These are spirits…"

Though they reacted differently, both of their eyes were glimmering. There were so many spirits, just like them. This would be great motivation for them.

"Falfa's gonna say hi to everyone!"

The ever-proactive Falfa quickly ran off and started talking to all the spirits. "Hello! I'm Falfa!"

She was so outgoing! More than I was when I was a kid, for sure!

In comparison, Shalsha was carefully observing the spirits. It didn't seem like she had the courage to go up and talk to them on her own. Wait, "no courage" was a weird way to put it. This was normal. Not even I would go up and talk to them outright.

"Shalsha, if you want to go around and say hello, I'll go with you." I stood to face her and squatted down. I was eye level with her now. "You were invited, so you can be as social as you want, okay?"

Shalsha didn't respond right away, but when she did, she said, "I want you…to come with me…Mom…"

"Okay. Let's make our rounds, then."

To be honest, I was thankful. I felt awkward going around to say hello as a non-spirit, and having Shalsha with me was giving me psychological support. In a way, our interests aligned.

But, betraying my expectations, Shalsha did as Shalsha was—a girl who really had it together.

"Good evening, I am Shalsha, a slime spirit… This is my first time attending…"

As she said her greetings, Shalsha handed over a card with her name written on it!

She's handing out business cards! Just like a Japanese businessman!

"Welcome to this gathering of spirits. I am Forahn, spirit of the falls."

"Jasva, spirit of volcanic ash."

"I'm Misami, spirit of cumulonimbus clouds."

The other spirits greeted her in turn. The categories were more specific than I thought…

"I am Azusa, Witch of the Highlands and mother of Shalsha. I'm here as her chaperone. Nice to meet you…"

I don't think I'll ever get used to introducing myself like this, no matter how old I get…

There was a stir.

"The Witch of the Highlands? You mean the one who decimated the blue dragons and the demons?!"

"I heard she's sent all sorts of adventurers to their graves."

"They say she's practically a god."

You're getting too worked up! I haven't decimated anyone! They're still living peacefully right now!

After I corrected them, they were still accepting of me.

"But you know, I never knew there were so many kinds of spirits," I said first to the lady waterfalls spirit.

"Yes. We are all rather divided by concept. Among the water spirits, there are puddle spirits, spring water spirits, underground water spirits, hot spring spirits, rivers, marshes, ponds, lakes, oceanic depths, everything."

"They sure are specific…"

"Well, if there were a general spirit of water, it would have to be really strong, right?"

"I understand what you want to say."

A spirit who ruled over all water would obviously have too much work. I guess even the most natural of beings had their limits.

"If you were wondering, slime spirits fall under the category of water spirits."

"What?! Is that true?!"

I'd lived with the two of them for a while, but I'd never thought about it!

"That's because slimes' bodies are apparently made of ninety-nine percent water. Thus, water spirits."

"But humans are made of seventy percent water, so most animals would fall under water's jurisdiction… Still, I get what you're saying."

Slimes were monsters, and I'd wondered how monster spirits worked. When I thought of them as a part of the water division, then it made sense.

"Shalsha and Falfa are water-type spirits…"

The news seemed to come as a shock to Shalsha herself, as she placed her hand to her chest and stared out into space.

"A water-type spirit… I feel like I've reached greater heights than before…"

"Definitely! It feels more dignified to say you're one of the water spirits than to say you're a slime spirit!"

Shalsha suddenly struck her hands out before her.

She reminded me of a middle schooler trying to awaken secret powers. Was she entering that phase?

"There's no water magic…"

"Maybe just being a water spirit alone isn't enough… We'll practice again, okay?"

Shalsha had used a specific spell for crushing evil to fight against me, and her mana had run completely dry ever since. Even if she learned some spells, she wouldn't be able to use them for decades.

Just discovering the truth about my daughters made it worth it enough to come here.

But I had still been underestimating what my daughters could do.

Shalsha rummaged through her bag and pulled something out.

What could it be? What could she produce after her business cards?

"I know this isn't much, but please take this as a symbol of our acquaintance. These are sweets called edible slimes and leaf slimes."

She was handing out gifts!!!

Seriously…? This girl wasn't bad at communication, either.

Falfa was also saying, "Here, some sweets for you!" and handing out edible slimes (eight packs) far away from us. They were kids, but I guess they had been alive for fifty years…

Though I wondered if spirits would actually eat the sweets, they took them with a word of thanks as if nothing was out of the ordinary. Well, my daughters ate cooked food, too.

After that, we went around greeting and chatting with all sorts of spirits.

But all we really talked about were things like where someone found a mountain with pretty flowers, which bakery had the best bread, or if there was really any point to spirits in the first place. Were they all really spirits?

Either way, we spent a few peaceful hours like that.

Along the way, we met up with Falfa, and the three of us went around to all the spirits. I thought they did a magnificent job as newcomers.

"This World Spirit Summit is so much fun!"

"You're right. Having an opportunity like this every once in a while isn't so bad— Wait." I realized something was odd here. "This summit hasn't started at all, has it?"

Indeed—I felt like it'd been almost two hours since the spirits first appeared, but nothing meeting-like seemed to be happening. This was outside, so maybe it was taking place at a different venue?

I went to the spirit of the falls, who I'd had a great conversation with earlier. I was the type to talk a lot to people once I got to know them.

"Excuse me, but will the meetings be starting soon? I heard this is where they'll be taking place..."

"...? I don't really understand your question. You're already participating."

Okay, but I don't understand what you're *saying.*

"I don't see anything that seems like a meeting. Is it already happening elsewhere?"

"Ohhh, I see. I see your mistake."

The spirit of the falls seemed to understand me. What was it?

"The World Spirit Summit is just a gathering for us spirits to get together and have a chat."

It was more slapdash than I thought!

It was more World Spirit Chitchat. *Summit* was overkill. There wasn't even a theme.

"Oh, and this World Spirit Summit should be ending soon. I'll see you next time, then. I'm not sure when or where the next one will be, though."

The spirit of the falls waved to me, walked a few steps away, then poofed into thin air. I guess she could teleport.

Shalsha looked a little disappointed after overhearing my conversation.

"To be honest, I wanted the concept to be a little clearer. I was excited to find out what we were going to talk about."

"That's because you're so conscientious, Shalsha. Well, these sorts of loose ties are also charming, in a way. I didn't see much of a hierarchy here."

Falfa was exercising her solid communication skills chatting with other spirits elsewhere, but I had a feeling the number of spirits here was starting to dwindle.

They were probably disappearing like the spirit of the falls did, and I could see some of them vanishing from the lake on foot.

The end of the event was coming closer, but we didn't even get an announcement to mark the beginning.

They just talked freely and went home at their leisure.

Shalsha must have accomplished what she set out to do, as she sat at the edge of the lake and took out a pack of edible slimes.

"You want one, Mom?"

"Sure, I'll have one. Let's stick around until Falfa's ready to go home."

"Okay."

As Shalsha stared out into space, I observed the remaining spirits. I couldn't really see anything special that set them apart from humans. It felt like I was attending the wedding of someone I didn't know well at all, then I ended up coming to the after-party.

It wasn't like I made a mistake or anything; it was okay. Things like this happened sometimes.

"But there's something that still bothers me," Shalsha said as she ate.

"What is it? What bothers you?"

"Even though this didn't have the format of a summit, someone sent us the information about the event. That means there has to be an executive office or something."

"I see... You think about a lot of things, don't you, Shalsha?"

Shalsha really was diligent... Who did she take after? I hadn't raised her from the very beginning, so maybe she'd been like that since she was born.

"I want to know who the sender is, at least, but—" Then, Shalsha's expression clouded over. "But so many people have gone already, I don't think it's possible..."

As I sat with Shalsha, the number of people dwindled still, and there were now only a handful left. That would be tough.

Soon there was no one else to talk to, and Falfa came over to us. She tossed an edible slime into her mouth.

"I guess it's over now."

"Yeah. Everyone's gone. We should head to the inn."

Just as I lifted my rear off the ground—

A single woman appeared right in front of us, in the middle of the lake.

She was probably a spirit, too.

"How was the World Spirit Summit? Ufufu~"

The question sounded like something someone from an executive committee would say.

And my very first impression of her was how big her boobs were. They were massive. Bigger than Halkara's. Halkara's were a healthy size, but these were too big. I bet if she closed her eyes and stood on one leg, she'd fall over because of them.

She had a generally calm air about her and soft, gentle-looking eyes.

"Falfa got to speak to a lot of spirits and had lots of fun!"

"I wanted the World Spirit Summit to be more like a summit."

The contrast between the girls was easy to see. I was indecisive, so my opinion sat squarely in the middle of theirs.

"Ufufu." She giggled. "I see~ It used to be more like a summit in the past. But then the spirits who weren't interested stopped coming, and attendance suffered~ So we decided to stop holding meetings~"

So spirits didn't want to attend a stuffy and formal event, either. Spirits were more lax than humans were, after all.

That was a general tendency, but long-lived races would start dropping the ball after so long.

"Oh, I forgot to introduce myself. I am a droplet spirit. There are lots of spirit children without names, but I am called Yufufu. I'm the one who sent the invitation~"

She'd come to talk to us, which meant that she was in charge of all the administrative stuff.

"A droplet spirit? What kind of spirit is that?"

"You know how water drips from the gutter after the rain, or how the water drips in spring as the snow melts? That's me—a droplet spirit."

These water types were crazy specific!

"The other spirits often call me a busybody. No one else would take on the administrative duties of the World Spirit Summit, so I did it myself. We held the summit in my neighborhood one time. They called me Momma," Yufufu said, placing her right hand against her cheek.

I could tell where the nickname came from. *Momma* suited her way better than *Ma* or *Mother Dearest* would.

And she wasn't like my own mom at all. Mine always said, *"That's fine for them but not for us."* Whenever I begged her for something my friends had, that was her favorite answer.

"And so, as I took on my administrative duties, I decided I may as well investigate all I could about spirits. See, spirits sometimes pop up out of nowhere. And I heard a rumor from a wind spirit that there were slime spirits, so that's why I sent the invitation to you."

"Not a *rumor on the wind* but a *rumor from a wind spirit!*"

Now that spirits were involved, the explanation suddenly made a lot more sense. I could see wind spirits liking gossip!

"Ever since I took charge of the World Spirit Summit, there have been many new participants."

If you're going to do one thing for a long time, you need new blood.

"Oh my, well, we can't stay chatting here forever, can we? Why don't you all come over to my home? If you don't have any place to stay, you're welcome to stay with me."

"Oh, that's tempting..."

The summit had been so mysterious that I'd checked the nearby inns, but I hadn't made any reservations.

"But I'm not a spirit, just a regular old witch. Is that okay...?"

"Of course. You don't have to refuse because of that! Ufufu~"

Just looking at Yufufu's face was kind of soothing.

"You're not Falfa's mommy but you look like a mommy... Why?" Falfa was starting to get confused.

Probably because the concept of "mother" was a broad one...

People could exude that motherly feel without actually being a parent...

"Big Sister, that's because people can still seem maternal without having children... Shalsha feels her motherliness, too..."

©Benio

Shalsha was bewildered, too. And so was I!

"Then hold on tight, okay? We'll fly using spiritual teleportation magic~," Yufufu said, then wrapped her arms around me. I put my arms around Falfa and Shalsha from behind them.

"Er, I don't think we need to be so close together…"

"Don't underestimate the power of physical contact."

As Yufufu's chest overwhelmed me, a strange feeling was born within me…like I was her child…

◇

We teleported, and before I knew it, we had arrived in a completely different place.

We were in a mountain with a small double-step waterfall. The second waterfall appeared right at the edge of the basin of the first. Next to the second waterfall's basin was Yufufu's house, right where healthy ferns grew everywhere under water that was dripping from the rock. There really were lots of water droplets everywhere.

From the way the interior was furnished, I wouldn't have been surprised to learn a regular person lived here. Even though she was a spirit, it seemed like she lived a human lifestyle.

"You still haven't eaten anything, have you? I can't make much more than a milk potage soup and pancakes right now, though. Wait a moment."

When I had a sip of the soup, a thought came to me:

"This tastes like home…"

An overwhelming gentleness flowed throughout my body. It was almost like the main ingredient…

The always-energetic Falfa sounded so gentle as she gave her appraisal, "My heart feels so warm…," with a peaceful expression. It was wholly calming.

"Oh, so nostalgic…," said Shalsha. "I almost feel homesick…" She actually started to shed some tears.

"I'm so happy to hear that."

Momma…I mean, Yufufu watched on with delight. The topic of spirits barely came up, but it didn't feel like we needed to talk about it here.

Afterward, the girls took a bath like normal and then went to bed and fell asleep as they always did.

I was still wide-awake, so I was drinking the hot honeyed water that Yufufu made for me.

"How is it?"

"Oh, it's nice, thank you."

"There's no need to be so polite. You've lived a long life, too."

"O-oh, okay…"

I knew what this felt like. This was like coming home to my parents.

"You know, the real reason I sent the invitation was because I was interested in you, Witch of the Highlands."

She readily laid out the truth.

"Why would you be interested in—? Well, I guess there are a number of reasons…"

I'd been a little unruly in a lot of places (figuratively, mostly, but sometimes for real).

The demons had taken an interest in me, so it wasn't too strange for spirits to do the same.

"Indeed. And your name started to spread so suddenly, no? I wanted to see what kind of person you were. And as the one in charge of the World Spirit Summit, I was also interested in little Falfa and Shalsha." Yufufu smiled faintly with her softly shaped eyes.

"And what'd you think of meeting the witch you were so interested in?"

"You're just as I expected. I can tell by watching the girls interact that you're building a beautiful family. You're a wonderful mother."

I had almost never been complimented like this before. I was tickled.

"I don't have any experience as a mom, but I think that's why I feel a responsibility to play the part as best I can. Without me, they would never have been born."

"But it's also clear that there's something you still lack."

What could it be? I didn't think she'd flunk me now, though.

"Azusa, what you don't have is a mother."

"…??? I'm sorry, but do you think you could be more specific…?"

Except Yufufu didn't seem to be joking.

Her gaze felt so warm. It was almost impossible to imagine that we'd just met.

"You are having a lovely time living in the house in the highlands with the girls."

"Yeah, and it's fun. It wasn't exactly painful living alone for three hundred years, but I learned that having housemates does have its good points."

I couldn't pick my preference, rank them, or compare them. They were just two completely different experiences.

"And the house in the highlands belongs to you, right? Which means you have to act as the lady of the house, I'm sure?"

"Well, yeah. I'm the one who was living there first…"

"Which means you don't have anyone to play the part of your mother in that house or anywhere nearby, no?"

When she mentioned it, I realized it.

It was obvious if you thought about it logically.

I was a transplant from another world; a witch I was born and a witch I'd always been.

I didn't have a mother here.

"Of course, there are plenty of children who live away from their mothers and many children who don't know who their mother is. Still, it's better to have one than not—don't you think?"

Since I'd truly lived freely and without care, I was never really indulged by anyone. I'd lived all this time without ever being aware of what I'd been missing.

"I mean, I get what you're trying to say, but I don't know how to deal with that…"

Who in the world would be my mom? I'd been alive for three hundred years.

Yufufu reached out to pat me on my chest. Really, I could just say she was patting my breasts.

"That's why, Azusa, if you're all right with it, why don't I be your mother?"

I paused. "……What?"

I didn't think this was a proposal I could immediately accept with a "Yes, please!"

You didn't get an offer like that every day…

"Erm… This is pretty embarrassing, and… Miss Yufufu, is there any advantage to this at all…?"

"Does there need to be one? I said I was a busybody, no? See, you might seem to have it all together in life, but you still want a mother at times. And when that happens, you are more than welcome to depend on me."

Nrrrgh… My mind was a mess because this was my first time experiencing something like this in my life. But just having someone be a mother for me could buoy me up. Some things you could talk about only with your mom, and sometimes people just wanted to be spoiled rotten…

"I-I'm not going to be sending you money because I'm your kid, okay…?"

"I don't need money. I just thought you might be pushing yourself sometimes."

Yufufu stood and spread out her arms.

"And that's when you can lean on me. You've been working very, very hard, Azusa."

What overpowering magnanimity… Unfortunately, I didn't have it yet—the power to validate someone unconditionally…! The power that only someone more senior in life could produce…!

Like a drunkard, I staggered toward Yufufu and buried my face in her chest.

Calling her by her first name would still put too much distance between us now.

Momma Yufufu!

"Momma… Momma Yufufu…"

This spirit was going to drag humans into depravity. But I was fine with that.

"I don't really have anything that's bothering me now, but can we stay like this for a little?"

"Yes. Stay there until you feel better. What do you want for breakfast tomorrow?"

I felt like my mind was melting. I also felt like a poison that had long infected my body was slowly being purified…

This was the power of a mother… A mysterious power of recovery…

I stayed cradled in Momma Yufufu's bosom for a long while.

I felt like I'd never wake up again if I fell asleep like this, but that wouldn't happen, right? She felt perfectly omnipotent and everything, but I didn't have to worry that much, right?

Afterward, I really did fall asleep, but my soul didn't end up stolen or anything, and I woke up in the bed in the morning.

Momma Yufufu sat in the chair by the bed, smiling.

"You're more like a saint than a spirit, Momma Yufufu…"

This was something I'd never experienced in my three hundred years of living.

There were still plenty of things that I knew nothing about.

"He-he-he, humans will always be someone's child. That is also true for you. And you may call me Momma anytime, okay?"

I felt like that was a line I couldn't cross as a person. I couldn't do that with other people around…

"It's all right. All you have to do if you don't have a mom is create one yourself."

I yielded.

"Momma Yufufu…"

My mind was still in a daze as I sat at Momma Yufufu's dining table.

I can't stay like this. I needed to get back to normal… I couldn't see my daughters the way I was now. I was still *their* mother, so I couldn't space out too much.

I stood before a mirror that was the perfect size for my face, checked my expression, and returned to parent mode.

All right, this should be good enough!

And then, Falfa and Shalsha came in.

"Good morning, you two! Did you sleep well?" I asked them brightly and energetically, like a dependable mom.

But there was something odd about their reactions.

"Mommy, what's wrong…?"

"You shouldn't say anything, Big Sister."

"But Falfa will worry about Mommy if I don't ask!"

Hmm? Is there something wrong with me?

Momma Yufufu didn't have the terrifying power to drain people's youth. I checked in the mirror already—nothing had changed.

"If there's something that's bothering you, you can tell me."

"See!"

"Okay. Then Shalsha will obey, too."

Really, what was going on?

"Mommy, did you wet the bed? You're a grown-up, but…"

Wet the bed? No way. I couldn't have—

I then noticed my lower half was soaked.

"It can't be! I couldn't have! This has to be a mistake!"

Shalsha almost never smiled, but a grin was spreading across her entire face.

"Mom, neither Shalsha nor Big Sister will make fun of the physical peculiarities of humans. You don't need to try so hard to hide it."

"Shalsha, I'm really glad you're growing up to be such a wonderful young lady, but I'm not trying to hide anything!"

"It happens. Falfa understands. It's okay!"

No! This is all wrong! But it is true that I'm soaked, so maybe...

Wait, no, not in my three hundred years of life has this ever happened before.

Could I think of anything?

Then, Momma Yufufu entered the room. I turned to look toward her with a pleading gaze.

"Oh my, my..."

She was covering her mouth, like she just saw something she didn't mean to!

"Well, these things happen. To each her own, I suppose."

"Okay, come on! That's not it!"

"Perhaps, in exchange for your strength, you received a physique that was prone to these things?"

"No! I haven't made a deal with the devil or anything like that!"

Momma Yufufu patted me on the head.

"I know this is a delicate subject, so you don't need to worry about it. You're not any less of a person because of this!"

She wasn't going to budge on the premise that I wet myself...? Did I really, though...? If it happened when I wasn't aware, then I couldn't say they were wrong because it just wasn't in *my* memory...

"But first, please, if you have a change of clothes, could you give them to me...?"

And then, Momma Yufufu started to chuckle. "I'm sorry for teasing you. You looked at me so gloomily, I just had to."

Oh, that was the response of a trickster.

"I'm a droplet spirit, remember? So when you're close to me, water begins to drip, it seems. That's why you look wet."

"Oh, phew. Then all the mysteries have been solved."

That sure is an ability that plays on your sense of shame... I'm going to have to change.

"How about that! It's not your fault after all, Mommy."

"Shalsha believed you from the start, Mom."

No you didn't, Shalsha. You were trying to console me.

But it still seemed like something was on Falfa's mind—what was it? There couldn't be any bigger problem than this.

We ate the breakfast that Momma Yufufu prepared for us.

"We don't want to get in your way, so we'll go once we're finished eating."

"Awww. You can stay as long as you like here; don't worry about bothering me. You can laze around in an empty room as you wish."

Wow, she really feels like a real mom at home! I do want to stay and just do nothing!

But if I stayed away from the house for a few days, Laika and the others would start to worry, and we couldn't have that.

"I'm sorry. We're going to go for now..."

"Oh yes, you can come visit anytime."

"Sure... We will..."

I'll quietly drop by whenever I want Momma Yufufu to dote on me.

The taste of her homemade cooking really soothed my soul.

"Mommy? There's something that Falfa doesn't really understand," Falfa said as she stabbed a vegetable with her fork.

"Yes, what is it?"

"It looked like you peed your pants, right? That's what happens when you hold on to Miss Yufufu, right?"

"Apparently so."

"When were you holding on to her like that?"

The food I was eating lost all its flavor.

Is this going to ruin her upbringing? Calm down, calm down. There's nothing wrong with it. But it was true that I was also embarrassed to say it out loud…

Momma Yufufu sat opposite me, smiling in delight as I scrambled for an answer.

"That's something you'll find out when you grow up~"

"Don't phrase it that way; they'll misunderstand!"

"It's nothing weird, dear. Adults sometimes want to be like children, too. I just helped her with that. Do you understand, little Falfa?" Yufufu said with loving eyes.

"Yeah! Falfa understands perfectly now! When Falfa's nervous and stuff, I want to hug Mommy really tightly, too!"

She understands. Good, I'm glad.

I was truly relieved.

When we finished our breakfast, we left Momma Yufufu's house.

On the way back, she brought us to the edge of the lake with her transport magic.

"Just come here if you ever want to visit again."

I nodded—and then, in a quiet voice, I said, "Bye-bye, Momma. Take care."

For the first time since living in this world for three hundred years, I had a momma.

After all, those three centuries brought me daughters—it wasn't strange to get a mom at all. Yep, I was in the clear!

That day, Beelzebub and the leviathan sisters Fatla and Vania visited the house in the highlands again.

These three were way too nonchalant about waltzing into people's homes. They brought gifts every time, but it was still way too often. Did they think my house was a bar or something? *This is a private residence, you know.*

"Ohhh, the meat in this stew is so tender. It falls right off the bone. It's so delightfully delicious!" Laika was thoroughly enjoying the dish Beelzebub brought along, and now it was even harder for me to complain…

"Right, right? I had Vania line up for half an hour in order to purchase this from one of the best side-dish shops in Vanzeld town!"

Beelzebub looked proud, but she really was ordering Vania around… *Vania should be the one acting proud, not you.*

Beelzebub left her seat and went to the toilet. She was in a great mood, since there was drink as well.

While she was gone, I posed a question to the two leviathans: "Hey, you two. Does Beelzebub actually do her work on the regular?"

She couldn't be the agricultural minister, as lax as she was… This might be a fantasy world, but she was still a government official.

"Our boss is fulfilling her duties well. The reason why I lined up at the shop was because I made a big mistake, and Boss cleaned up my mess for me. This was my thanks."

"You don't sound very convincing, Vania… I wonder if someone a little more serious will tell me about it…"

"What! I'm shocked!"

Hey, you're the one who just said you made a big mistake!

"I admire Lady Beelzebub. She is very busy when she's on the clock. She would not have been able to work as the agricultural minister for so long if not."

"If you say the same, Fatla, then it might be true, but it's hard to imagine. I've never seen her working…"

"I understand completely."

So she did see it. At the very least, that meant that Beelzebub's apparently irresponsible behavior when she came here wasn't just me.

"And if I might offer you a suggestion"—a small smile appeared on Fatla's lips—"if you like, you're more than welcome to observe Lady Beelzebub as she works."

Oh, it was like a classroom observation. Or a work observation, rather.

"That's an interesting idea, but wouldn't Beelzebub hate it? She'd never give me the okay. I'd say no if I was in her position…"

"You don't need permission. You can use all sorts of magic, can't you, Miss Azusa? What about invisibility?"

I opened my eyes wide, and not because of the underhanded idea itself.

"Fatla, I never thought *you'd* suggest something like that…"

"I want to try playing tricks, too, on occasion." Fatla chuckled like a little imp. Oh right, position-wise, this girl was a government official. She was far from an innocent girl—the opposite, in fact.

"Fine. I can't use invisibility magic, but I'll learn it through spell creation. Once I can use it, we can discuss more in detail. And everyone else who heard this, not a word."

Flatorte and Laika nodded.

Just then, Beelzebub came back.

"Well then, shall we open another bottle? Mm... The room is rather quiet. Did you not talk about anything?"

"The conversation just dies off sometimes."

Beelzebub, of course, didn't seem to suspect anything. She was drunk anyway.

While Beelzebub went off to Falfa and Shalsha's room, we formulated our plot.

I had learned invisibility magic without any incident, and now the show could begin.

The day before we put our plan into action, I rode on Laika to Vanzeld Castle.

I spent the night, and then the next morning, I met up with Fatla. It was perfect, since Laika went off to train with Fighsly.

"Now then, Miss Azusa, I'll take you to the department of agriculture."

"Okay. Just in case, I'll go invisible now."

I made myself disappear with my new spell.

The front entrance of the agricultural ministry building where the demons worked was enough to tell me it was luxurious. The decorations were over-the-top, too. It looked sort of gothic.

Inside, demons sat with documents and chatted with coworkers.

The whole atmosphere was electric.

"Pass that on to Kaltenta in the personnel department!" "I got orders to go on a business trip, so can someone cover for me in next week's meeting?!" "We're having a meeting on the growth promotion of grapes in the meeting room in an hour!"

The workers were a diverse bunch, all demons, and they were each working their hardest...

There were no computers here, but otherwise, it wasn't much

different from my own company. No, some demons were staring hard at stone tablets with data displayed on them, so even that was practically identical.

"This is the agricultural planning division. They're a rather busy bunch."

Fatla seemed to be aware of where I was even though I was invisible, and she explained to me.

"I see... Everyone's working hard."

I'd end up like a spy if I kept peeking in rooms that weren't any of my business, so we went straight to where Beelzebub was.

When we came to the top floor, we found the door to the minister's room.

"Lady Beelzebub is carrying out her government duties beyond this door."

"Well, well, well. Let's see what she's up to."

Fatla slowly opened the door. It would be obviously strange if my invisible self opened it, so I slipped in as she did so.

And then—

"Vania, all the documents you created have last year's date on them... You will have to go and re-receive all the approval signatures!"

"What! Please, Boss!"

Beelzebub was pointing out one of Vania's misses to her.

"And right out of the gate, my sister makes a blunder... How embarrassing..." Fatla pressed a hand to her head.

Her own sister wasn't even hiding how embarrassed she was...

"Oh, Fatla, go to the meeting this afternoon. The more heads the better, since these are talks with other ministries."

As she called out to Fatla, I quickly moved to the corner of the room.

She'd find out if I wandered around too much, so I'd keep this position.

"Hmm. I thought I heard something..." Beelzebub was sharp...

"A larger demon must be coming up the stairs."

"Okay. Now then, I've reviewed all the documents marked for

submission at the end of the month, so I'm moving on. The auditing office hasn't given us any lip so far this fiscal year, so that's easy. They're all massive sadists, that lot."

"Understood. I shall get through a little more work until my next meeting, then."

And so I began my real observations.

The minister's room was big, but the only ones working there were Beelzebub, Fatla, and Vania. The leviathan sisters apparently took on a secretarial role.

I had doubted if she was really taking her job seriously, but to be honest, I got my answer in the first three minutes.

Beelzebub's eyes were deadly serious—she was 100 percent in business mode.

She quickly checked over her documents, and if she had a question, she would either add a tag to it or order Vania, "Ask what's going on here budget-wise."

Minister wasn't just a title, then. She was working really hard. Her competence was almost tangibly oozing from her.

After thirty minutes, I ran into a big problem.

I'm so bored...

When I thought about it, what Beelzebub was doing was office work. Hours and hours of this weren't going to make it any more interesting!

There were almost two hours until lunch... This was painful...

Beelzebub suddenly stood up.

"The air in this room feels different from normal—almost as though there are extra people..."

So she could tell, even though I was invisible...

"There's no one else here, Boss! It's not like an invisible person is hiding anywhere, you know."

Hey! Vania! Don't say what we agreed on out loud like that!

Beelzebub carefully scanned the room. I covered my mouth with my hand and held my breath!

"It feels like part of the air flow in here disappeared... As though someone's holding their breath..."

She was really sharp! This was difficult, even though I was invisible and hidden.

"Lady Beelzebub, please stop spouting nonsense and return to your work."

"You're right. I have plenty of things to do."

Fatla jumped in for me. *Thank you, Fatla!*

Also, now that I'd learned that Beelzebub was a real business-woman, I wanted to go home. But she wasn't leaving her seat, so I couldn't say anything to Fatla.

Staff would occasionally come in to bring documents, and I could leave when that happened, but it would be rude to leave without saying anything to Fatla or Vania...

If I'd known this would happen, I would've brought something along to pass the time...

Without any other choice, I lay down on the carpet and stared off into space.

Most of her work was drab. Maybe I should've picked the evening to watch her work...

As I lay on the floor, it finally came time for lunch.

The ringing of the break bell echoed throughout the building.

"Phew! Time for a rest."

Beelzebub stood and stretched. She also unfurled her wings. I guess they needed stretching, too.

"Today's a day you made lunch, isn't it, Vania?"

"Yes! I've created something colorful using seasonal ingredients! I call it A Colorful Lunch Using Seasonal Ingredients!"

"I didn't ask for the name."

Ohhh, the secretary brought in handmade lunch. That's a nice system.

Had someone brought in lunch for me when I was a corporate slave,

I probably would've been healthier; maybe I would have stayed alive. There was no love in convenience store lunches.

But I was facing an even greater problem than I had before.

If I couldn't leave the room, then I wouldn't be able to eat lunch...

This is hard... I at least want to munch on a cookie...

And at the perfect timing, my stomach grumbled loudly.

Crap! I couldn't win against physiological phenomena!

"Who was that? How hungry are you? Your stomach is much too assertive."

"It was not me."

"Then by process of elimination, it had to be Vania."

"It wasn't me! That sound was the Wi—which was much too violent; it was not something my stomach could make."

Vania almost said "Witch of the Highlands"! The recovery was a little forced, but she pulled it off, at least!

"It is not I, either. It sounded too much like that of an idiot's to be mine. Mine growls much more nobly."

Hey! That's a weird thing to dis me for!

I wanted to protest, but I couldn't!

"Well, whose stomach it was matters not. The growling will stop when we are full."

Urgh... I can't eat, though...

Vania produced a bag for carrying the lunches.

"This is mine; this is for you, Boss; and this is for Big Sis; and this is for the Wi—" Vania went pale.

"Why did you bring lunch for four people?" Fatla looked at Vania like she was an idiot. She really was a screwup!

"And what is a *Wi*?"

"Wi... Which I have prepared, an extra. Yes! An extra in case anyone wants to eat any more!"

"Uh... If no one eats it, then it becomes waste... Did you not think about this beforehand...?"

Beelzebub was cornering her with sound arguments!

"A-actually...I made too much! So I made a fourth one... That's all... There is absolutely no other reason why..."

Sweat was dripping from Vania's forehead.

Watching her, Beelzebub seemed to figure something out.

"I see, I see. I couldn't bear to have it go to waste, so I suppose I'll take it to another room and ask if anyone else wants it. Oh, if only there was a fourth person in this room, but of course there isn't! Now then, I'm off to search for someone who wants this lunch! In another room!"

I canceled my invisibility magic. "Ahhh, please! Please! I'll eat it! Don't take it away!"

Beelzebub looked at me, annoyed. "I knew it. I knew something was odd in here."

Afterward, I explained my situation to her. Now that she knew I was here, explaining everything was my responsibility.

"—And so, I wanted to see if you were really working," I said as I ate my lunch. It was really good. The lunch was innocent, but Vania? Not so much.

Fatla and Vania both looked a little guilty. They couldn't just shake this one off.

"And so? I am working splendidly, am I not?" Beelzebub crowed.

"Yeah... You were serious. So serious, watching you was mind-numbing."

"Have you ever heard of office work that makes for an entertaining show? I am not working to amuse you!"

"You're right... I won't do this again... Now I know you're an upstanding participant in society..."

"Mm-hmm. And see to it that this doesn't happen again. I will let it slide this time, but in the future, you will submit an application before-hand. We can create a fun and informative field trip for visitors. Even better with the help of the PR department." Beelzebub handed me an application form.

"Er, I appreciate the goodwill, but I'm not really interested in the agricultural ministry's work, so..."

"Falfa and Shalsha may want to have the experience, so take it home. Actually, bring them with you!"

She's so shrewd when it comes to them!

Now that she'd seen through my evil deed, I had no choice but to tap into Falfa's and Shalsha's thoughts on a field trip to the ministry.

A few days later, my daughters went on a field trip to the department of agriculture.

And they had a great time.

The End

This is Kisetsu Morita—it's been a while!

I have now safely delivered Volume 4 of *I've Been Killing Slimes...* to you!

Volume 1 came out in January, Volume 2 came out in April, Volume 3 came out in July, and now Volume 4 is out in October—I'm glad they're being published at such a fast pace. This is all thanks to those of you who are purchasing them. Thank you very much!

Now, in this volume, we've had a new character appear who we'd call an unsuccessful band member (well, she's working on her own, so she's not strictly a "band"). That is Kuku, the bunny-eared girl.

There is an element of real life in her story.

I currently live in the west side of Tokyo, but a few years ago, I lived in Fukui Prefecture.

There, I met an unsuccessful band member.

His musical work didn't go so well in Tokyo, so he came back to his home in Fukui. He stopped playing music and was trying to find a proper job. He talked to me about this.

To me, it felt like he had no ambition; I could feel it rolling off him: "I *guess* I'll look for work now."

So I said to him, "You still seem to have regrets, so why don't you settle that however you see fit before moving on to the next thing? You need money, of course, but this is your only life... Aren't you going to regret it if you just start working now?" (Something like that.)

In the end, he thanked me a lot.

I don't know what happened to his music after that, but it's at least true that he realized how lost he was, and I think that itself was a good thing.

Also, there's no theme like that behind Pondeli, the ex-NEET, but there are probably people who have a similar history. Someone who used to be a shut-in NEET like that is now working very hard as an author.

I also know people who didn't even have a place to live at one point but overcame that situation and are now working at some major enterprise. That sort of sounds like Halkara.

And so, the contents of this story are generally leisurely, but if you think about it, many of the characters here were on the brink of a downfall.

Now that I mention it, your very own author Morita has been just about to fall many times but just barely managed to find footing. Now I've gotten all the way here...

I want to continue writing the series about happy lives for these kinds of characters, so if any of my readers are going through tough times, then I hope this series can lift your spirits, even just a millimeter.

We'll leave our serious talk there for now and go into announcements and acknowledgments.

First, you can find the comic version and spin-offs in GanGan GA! I'll paste the URL here! You can read it all for free, of course!

http://www.ganganonline.com/contents/slime

Thanks to you, the initial views of the first chapter reached a record high in the history of GanGan GA... It feels like this has reached heights I never imagined...

I give my heartfelt thanks to the illustrator, Yusuke Shiba-sensei! Azusa's personality is so much clearer than in the original! (Wait, if it's clearer than the original, then that's my problem...)

Even my very critical friends in the manga industry texted me to say, "It's a really great comic adaptation!" And my non-nerdy classmates from college were texting me their thoughts on the comic. I really felt like it had a reach on a totally different level.

The spin-off also illustrates Beelzebub's past, which we've never seen in the main story—or, rather, is very hard to portray in Azusa's first-person view. This also reached record-breaking page views on the GanGan GA short story section. I'm so happy! If I can expand even more on the *I've Been Killing Slimes...* world from here on out, I could not be any happier as the author!

Also, when the fifth volume comes out in January, there will be a version that comes bundled with a drama CD! And do you know what that means??? That means Azusa and Laika and the others will get voices!

I'm so excited to see what sort of voice everyone will get! And I might have the chance to meet the voice actors, so I'm really excited about that, too! (I'm serious!)

A sincerest thank-you to Benio-sensei, who created wonderful illustrations this time around, too! As the volumes go on, Azusa and company are growing more and more at home in the highlands, and the pictures are starting to look less like insert illustrations and more like snapshots of real life. I can't wait to see what you produce next!

And I have never been more thankful to all the fans who've been following the book series so far! Thanks to everyone, the series is proceeding very well.

Just as this book goes on sale, I'll be reaching my tenth anniversary as an author. I've somehow kept this up for quite a while now. I will be more than happy if I can make something that everyone can enjoy.

And so, we will meet again in January, when the fifth volume with the drama CD (there will also be normal versions without the CD) goes on sale!

Kisetsu Morita